Summer Bride

Holiday Brides, Book 2
A Sweet Western Romance
by
USA Today Bestselling Author
SHANNA HATFIELD

Wholesome Hearts

PUBLISHING

Summer Bride
Holiday Brides Book 2

ISBN: 978-1723321375

For permission requests, please contact the author, with a subject line of "permission request" at the e-mail address below or through her website.
shanna@shannahatfield.com

This is a work of fiction. Names, characters, businesses, places, events, and incidents either are the product of the author's imagination or are used in a fictitious manner. Any resemblance to actual persons, living or dead, business establishments, or actual events is purely coincidental.

Published by Wholesome Hearts Publishing, LLC.
wholesomeheartspublishing@gmail.com

*To the selfless who give their best
to helping others.*

Books by Shanna Hatfield

FICTION

<u>**CONTEMPORARY**</u>

Holiday Brides
Valentine Bride
Summer Bride
Easter Bride
Lilac Bride
Lake Bride

Rodeo Romance
The Christmas Cowboy
Wrestlin' Christmas
Capturing Christmas
Barreling Through Christmas
Chasing Christmas
Racing Christmas
Keeping Christmas
Roping Christmas
Remembering Christmas

Grass Valley Cowboys
The Cowboy's Christmas Plan
The Cowboy's Spring Romance
The Cowboy's Summer Love
The Cowboy's Autumn Fall
The Cowboy's New Heart
The Cowboy's Last Goodbye

Summer Creek
Catching the Cowboy
Rescuing the Rancher
Protecting the Princess
Distracting the Deputy

Women of Tenacity
Heart of Clay
Heart of Hope
Heart of Love

<u>**HISTORICAL**</u>

Pendleton Petticoats
Dacey	*Lacey*
Aundy	*Bertie*
Caterina	*Millie*
Ilsa	*Dally*
Marnie	*Quinn*
	Evie

Pendleton Promises
Sadie

Baker City Brides
Tad's Treasure
Crumpets and Cowpies
Thimbles and Thistles
Corsets and Cuffs
Bobbins and Boots
Lightning and Lawmen
Dumplings and Dynamite

Hearts of the War
Garden of Her Heart
Home of Her Heart
Dream of Her Heart

Hardman Holidays
The Christmas Bargain
The Christmas Token
The Christmas Calamity
The Christmas Vow
The Christmas Quandary
The Christmas Confection
The Christmas Melody
The Christmas Ring
The Christmas Wish

Chapter One

"What's a guy got to do to get a girl in this town?"

The men around Justin James stopped working and burst into uncontrollable laughter.

Shocked by their reaction to his query, he looked up from the conduit he was in the midst of bending and glared at the construction crew. As the electrician hired for Golden Skies Retirement Village's new wing and therapy center, he'd spent the last two weeks around the crew working on the project. Until that moment, he'd considered them friends. Now they approached enemy status.

"You ever thought about getting a little work done?" one of the men asked in a mocking tone. "If you try being someone other than yourself, maybe it would help."

"Yeah, you might want to step up your game,

like taking a shower once in a while," another joked.

Those who hadn't already left for the day chuckled and guffawed, stirring Justin's temper. Under normal circumstances, Justin was easy-going and affable. But the ongoing hilarity about a problem he wanted addressed was about to wear his patience dangerously thin.

"What's so funny?" he asked, drawing more amusement at his expense. The men looked like dusty bobble-headed bozos as they doubled over with mirth, hardhats nearly crashing together as they wheezed and chortled.

"I don't have a problem finding girls around here," a man named Joe said when he finally stopped laughing.

A stocky construction guy named Tim snorted and pointed at Joe. "You find them, Joe, but it's keeping them where you run into trouble. Didn't you just finalize your divorce from wife number four?"

"Three, but who's counting," Joe said, glaring at Tim. He turned his attention back to Justin. "Maybe you should lower your standards."

Not that Justin had exceptionally high expectations to begin with, but his catalog of requirements was reasonable for a woman to be considered dating material. His checklist was simple: clean, groomed, IQ higher than dirt, self-efficient, nice, friendly, and a sense of humor. He counted it as a bonus if the woman was attractive, gainfully employed, and possessed good manners.

"My standards are just fine," Justin said

defensively. He wished he'd never voiced the thoughts that had been running through his head as they finished up their work for the evening.

One of the first things he'd noticed when he'd moved to the small Eastern Oregon town of Holiday a week before Thanksgiving was the lack of eligible females.

"There are lots of unmarried women here at Golden Skies," Tim said, causing another round of laughter.

Widowed women ranging in age from seventy to nearly one hundred resided at the retirement village. They were definitely not dating material. He had enough trouble keeping the old women at bay as it was.

A few times he'd been in the lobby waiting to speak to the director of Golden Skies when he was nearly accosted by one of the residents. A woman named Matilda Dale seemed to think it was her job to squeeze his biceps and bat her eyes at him. The flamboyant outfits she wore combined with her round black-framed glasses made her look like Harry Potter's demented granny. From the stories he heard, she was as wacky as her appearance indicated.

"Maybe you should try dating your own species. I heard they have an abundance of dogs at the rescue kennel in town," Joe deadpanned.

Justin knew the guys were trying to be funny, but their teasing irritated him. Normally, he would have joined in their jollity, but right now he wanted to give Joe a black eye. Or two.

Finally, one of the men noticed the somber

expression on Justin's face and curtailed his amusement.

"Boss, are you serious?" asked Matt Smith, Justin's apprentice electrician and friend.

"Dead serious." Justin glanced over the group of men again before he returned his attention to the conduit. "Just forget I asked."

"No, dude." A man everyone called Bull thumped Justin on the shoulder, nearly toppling him to the floor.

Although he was six-feet tall in his sock-feet, Justin had to look up to Bull. He assumed the man's nickname derived from his massive size and not the fact he often told wild tales no one believed, but enjoyed all the same.

"It's a fair question," Bull said, looking at the others with a warning glare.

The men quieted and glanced at Justin again.

He shrugged. "In the few months I've lived here, I've gone out on exactly three disastrous dates. One gal conveniently forgot to mention she was married until her husband showed up at the pizza place and threatened to shoot us both. The second woman I took out never stopped talking the entire time I was stuck with her. She got shushed so many times at the movie theater, it's a wonder they didn't ask us to leave. I thought my ears might start bleeding before I called it a night. And the third was a doozy. The woman should be committed to a psycho ward, and I'm not joking. By the time we finished dinner, she was already talking about moving in with me and had picked out names for the three children she decided we'd have. When she demanded we drive to my place so she could analyze the demonic forces of the house, I couldn't get away from her fast enough."

A few chuckles rolled out of the men, but they gave Justin sympathetic looks.

"We've all been there, man," Bull said, and thumped him on the shoulder again. "Don't give up yet. There are some good women in town, too. Have you tried hanging out at The Blue?"

Justin shook his head. "The bar scene isn't really my thing, but thanks for sharing that tip, Bull."

The man nodded his head and looked to the others as they gathered their tools. "What about the grocery store? Women are always there."

"I tried picking up a girl there once," Tim said, grinning at the group. "I bumped into her cart on purpose to get her attention. I broke a dozen eggs and bruised her bananas. By the time she got done verbally dressing me down, I decided I didn't need a date that bad."

"How about the gas station?" Joe asked, yanking off his gloves and stuffing them in his back pocket. "You could be a hero and wash a windshield or two while the attendant pumps their gas."

With great effort, Justin refrained from rolling his eyes. "No, thanks. I don't have time for that, anyway."

"You could always join the PTA and hang out at the meetings. There are oodles of women there," Tim said with a mocking grin.

"Man, are you nuts?" Matt asked. "Most of the

women attending meetings at the school are married. The ones who aren't are like wild animals attacking fresh meat when a single guy shows up."

"Don't forget if they are there, they've most likely got a kid or two, or six," Bull added.

Justin swallowed down an exasperated sigh. "Thanks for all that awesome advice," he said in a voice heavy with sarcasm. "Isn't it time for you jokers to leave for the day?"

"Yeah, it is," Bull said, gathering his things along with the rest of the crew. "Don't work too late."

"I won't. See you guys tomorrow." Justin waved at them as they left.

"Want me to help you with that conduit?" Matt asked as he prepared to leave.

"No. I'm just gonna finish this one piece and then I'll call it a night. Enjoy your evening, Matt."

"I will, boss," Matt said, picking up his lunch box and giving Justin a studying look. "Are you really trying to find a girl?"

Justin refused to say anything further on the subject after the guys offered so many unhelpful suggestions. "Nah, it's all good."

"If you really want to meet someone, my sister has a friend who just moved back to town. She's divorced, but no kids."

Justin glanced over his shoulder at Matt and tossed him a grin. "Maybe you should take her out, then."

Matt laughed. "Maybe I will. See you in the morning."

Justin finished with the piece of conduit then

gathered his tools, pulled on his coat, and made sure everything was secured before he left for the evening.

As he walked through the cold drizzle of rain to his pickup, he thought about what the guys had said. He might not be the most handsome guy in the world, but Justin knew he was reasonably good looking. In spite of what was mentioned about him stepping up his game and attending to personal hygiene, Justin knew the guys were only joking. Of them all, he was the most well-groomed, at least most of the time.

His hand brushed over the stubble on his jaw and he tried to remember when he had last shaved. Maybe it was Monday? Or was it Sunday? It didn't really matter since he wouldn't be kissing anyone that night — or any night in the foreseeable future.

Until he moved to Holiday, he'd never had trouble getting a date, so he didn't think it was his personality.

He certainly wouldn't consider lowering his standards. After all, slightly dipping them had been the reason for the three horrible dates he'd endured.

Justin unlocked his pickup, set his tool bag on the backseat, and then climbed behind the wheel. He started the truck and let it warm up a minute to chase away the late February chill before he made his way home.

The one woman in town who had captured his interest turned out to be married. In fact, she worked right there at Golden Skies as the front desk receptionist. He'd seen Sage Presley around town a few times and had wondered about her, then the first time he set foot in the retirement village she'd greeted him with a warm, friendly smile.

Sage was everything he was looking for in a woman. She was sweet with the most intriguing green eyes. Her golden hair was thick and curly. Flawless skin and an amazing figure appeared model-worthy. And her beauty seemed to be far deeper than the surface. He'd seen her patiently and lovingly provide assistance to the residents of Golden Skies.

Eager to seize the opportunity to ask her out, he happened to notice a silver band on her ring finger before he blurted out a request to take her on a date. Then, much to his surprise, he'd watched her hug a boy who had to be entering his teen years and ask him if he was ready to go home. Justin overheard her inquiring about homework and how his day at school had been.

Either Sage had incredible genes that made her look far younger than her years, or she'd had a son at an unbelievably young age. If he had to guess, he would have pegged her as being in her early to mid-twenties. She had to be older, though, especially with a boy that big. Since Justin was almost twenty-eight, he didn't mind a woman being a little older, although he wasn't sure he wanted to get involved with someone who had a child. Being a parent to a teen wasn't something he'd considered. Then again, Sage was already taken so it was a moot point.

Justin didn't know what it was, but he was tired of playing the field, tired of trying to figure out the ever-changing rules to the games people played while dating. He just wanted to find someone special to share his life with. Someone who made him look forward to coming home every night. Someone he could wrap his arms around and love with all his heart.

Determined to change the direction of his thoughts, Justin pulled out of the parking lot and decided to run by the grocery store on his way home. Who knew? Maybe he'd bump into a woman there, although he had no intention of stooping to underhanded tactics like cart crashing just to meet a girl.

Humor restored, he chuckled as he recalled the conversation he'd just had with the guys. Joining the PTA? He absolutely was not that desperate.

At least not yet.

Chapter Two

"Yes, Mrs. Freemont. The activity bus departs at nine in the morning," Sage Presley assured a resident of Golden Skies Retirement Village given to worry. "We have your name on the list, so the bus won't leave without you."

Mrs. Freemont stopped wringing her hands together and sighed with relief. "Good. I don't want to miss the quilt show. It's wonderful a whole bus of us will get to enjoy it. I better make sure my outfit is pressed and ready to go. Good night, Sage." The woman hurried across the lobby toward the elevator.

"Good night, Mrs. Freemont." Sage tamped down the urge to giggle as she watched Mrs. Freemont sashay onto the elevator. Mrs. Freemont was a thin, petite woman naturally endowed with a chest that could have put Dolly Parton to shame.

Sage wondered how the poor dear managed to maintain her balance.

The previous month, Matilda Dale and Ruth Beaumont, two residents who seemed to have a bent for matchmaking and stirring up trouble, borrowed a bright red brassiere from Mrs. Freemont. The two scheming women used it as a flag, waving it outside the window of an apartment upstairs during a plot meant to bring Matilda's granddaughter and Ruth's nephew together.

In spite of their unorthodox methods, their efforts paid off since Fynlee and Carson had just returned from their honeymoon a few days ago. Sage had been friends with Fynlee ever since Matilda moved into Golden Skies. The older woman had been deemed crazy by many, but Sage knew Matilda merely owned a unique way of expressing herself through colorful clothes and sometimes questionable behavior. Fynlee doted on her grandmother and Ruth, who happened to be Matilda's best friend.

Sage enjoyed the front row seat she'd had to watch Fynlee fall in love with Carson, since they were often at the retirement village. The cowboy, who took over Ruth's ranch after her husband passed away, appeared equally besotted with his bride.

Fynlee had recently begun working at Golden Skies as an occupational therapist. Sage often took her lunch break with Fynlee and joined her as she ate with Matilda and Ruth. The conversations that took place around the table often kept her smiling all afternoon.

With her stress-filled life, Sage needed all the lighthearted moments she could get.

She tossed a quick glance at the clock on the wall across from her desk. It hung above the doorway to a library that smelled of books and, occasionally, menthol. The room boasted golden oak paneling and dark green embossed wallpaper with a pale green and mauve floral-patterned plush carpet. In addition to an incredible assortment of books, there were overstuffed chairs, and several small tables throughout the room, providing ample places to read and relax.

Golden Skies truly was a lovely facility, one where residents could feel independent but receive care if they needed it. There was a large gathering room where residents could visit if they chose. They also had a music room, a beauty parlor, a movie theater, and of course a cafeteria that served three nutritious meals each day.

Many of the residents had their own apartments where they could cook if they so desired. Most residents had smaller rooms with refrigerators and microwaves, but no stoves.

The new wing being constructed would add thirty rooms for residents who needed constant nursing care. There would also be an expanded medical area and a new therapy center.

Thoughts of the construction area made Sage's mind wander to one of the hunky guys she'd noticed. Several of the men were nice looking, but one in particular had caught her eye. She'd first seen him around Holiday before Christmas, then he'd stepped into the lobby one afternoon and asked to speak with the director of Golden Skies about the new wing being constructed. He told her he was the electrician hired for the project.

Justin James was tall and muscular with dark brown hair and warm brown eyes that lit up when he smiled. In fact, when he'd smiled at her that day, she'd been glad she was sitting at her desk. Unexpectedly, her knees felt like they were made of the pudding the cooks served in the cafeteria. She thought she'd sensed a bit of interest from him, but she wouldn't encourage it. Not when her life was already too full, too busy, and far too chaotic to even consider a relationship.

Who was Sage kidding? She refused to even allow herself to go on a casual no-strings-attached date. Between work and raising her brother, she had all she could handle at the moment.

Sage looked at the silver band on her left ring finger. The ring served the purpose of giving men the wrong impression that she was taken. It kept her from having to offer explanations or make excuses for the most part when men asked her out and she had to refuse.

The day Justin had lingered at her desk she'd been grateful her brother had arrived at the precise moment when the handsome electrician had moved closer and looked as though he intended to say something flirty. The sight of Shane had caused him to snap his mouth shut and step away.

She knew many people assumed between the ring on her finger and the thirteen-year-old in her care, that she was married with a child, or at least had been married. There were days that assumption pricked at her self-image, since she was only eleven years older than Shane. However, she supposed since she'd been raising him from the time she was eighteen, she probably looked and acted older than her age.

Sage knew she shouldn't care what people thought or assumed. Her attention should be focused on doing her job and making sure Shane grew up to be a good person. A few years down the road, when he was enrolled in college, would be soon enough to allow herself to think about her life and what she wanted to do with it.

Another glance at the clock on the wall assured her it was time to leave for the day. She'd just turned off her computer and slipped on her coat when Ruth and Matilda breezed off the elevator.

"Sage, darling!" Matilda said in a loud theatrical tone that rang across the lobby. "I'm so glad we caught you!"

Sage draped a scarf around her neck as she smiled at the two women. "What can I do for you?"

"Oh, she's leaving, Tilly," Ruth said in a soft, cultured voice. Sage admired Ruth's gentle ladylike manner. The woman always looked like she was ready for a garden party, even in the midst of winter. Ruth turned to Matilda and placed a hand on her arm. "Let's leave her be."

"No, Ruth. I'm happy to help if there is something I can do for you and Matilda." Sage had no idea what request would spill out of Matilda's lips, but they generally proved to be interesting.

"If you're quite sure, dear, we have the most unbelievable craving for grilled cheese sandwiches and tomato soup from the deli. Would you mind, terribly, going to pick up our order for us? Of course, we'd pay for soup and sandwiches for you and Shane, too."

Sage gave them an indulgent smile. "That's not necessary, ma'am. I'm happy to run the errand for you, though. It won't take me long."

"Wonderful!" Matilda clapped her hands, sending the dozen bracelets on her arm into a cacophonous symphony. Sage had noticed earlier the sweater Matilda wore looked like she'd been mauled by one of The Muppets and come out the victor. Bright orange fluffy yarn encircled Matilda's slight form from neck to mid-thigh. Turquoise leggings and bright red sparkly shoes completed the ensemble. One would never say Matilda Dale lacked daring when it came to fashion, or most areas of her life.

Although Sage thought it would be wonderful to grow up to be a fine lady like Ruth, she could see Matilda wrestled the most fun out of life with her "I don't care what you think, this is who I am" attitude.

The two women, so vastly different in personality and appearance, were the dearest, closest friends, though, and had been for years and years. Perhaps that adage about opposites attract extended to friendships, too.

"We don't want to be an inconvenience to you, dear," Ruth said, offering Sage a kindly look.

"It's no trouble at all. I promise. If you call in your order, it should be ready by the time I get there." Sage picked up her purse and took out her car keys and cell phone. "I'll send Shane a text to let him know I'll be home soon, then pick up your dinner. So just the two orders?"

"No, there are eight of us getting together for soup and sandwiches," Ruth said, handing Sage an envelope. "Our money is all in there."

"And we insist on paying for dinner for you and Shane, too." Matilda squeezed Sage's hands between hers.

Experience had taught Sage it was pointless to argue with Matilda, so she nodded her head. "Thank you. I'll be back as soon as I can."

"We know you will, darling. Drive safely in that nasty rain out there. At least it's above freezing. Otherwise it would be a real mess."

"Yes, it would," Sage agreed. She couldn't wait for spring and warmer weather to arrive. Not that she looked forward to having to take care of the lawn at the small house she rented, but she did anticipate the warmth of the sun on her face and the smell of flowers in the air.

She sent Shane a text that she'd be a few minutes late, but she'd bring dinner with her. Unable to stop herself, she reminded him to get his homework finished and to stop playing on his cell phone. Although she thought he was too young to have one, it had proved handy when she got it for him for his tenth birthday. It was easy to keep track of him that way, and so far he'd mostly followed her rules for keeping the phone. If nothing else, it gave her a good bargaining chip when she needed to threaten to take something away from him as a form of punishment.

Shane was a good kid, but he'd had a rough start to life. Considering they shared half of the same faulty gene pool, it wasn't like he didn't have the odds stacked against him. Thankfully, he was a strong student, even if he hated school. He'd pitched a colossal fit about going back to school after the holidays, but Sage had laid down the law and he'd gone, albeit begrudgingly. She didn't know why he hated school so much, and he refused to talk about it.

She assumed a portion of the problem rested in the fact he didn't have many friends. Shane was a loner by nature and the other kids sometimes teased him about living with his sister and not having parents. As Shane grew older, she worried about him getting into serious trouble. Right now, he occasionally skipped a class, sometimes behaved disrespectfully toward certain teachers, and frequently acted like everything wrong in his life was somehow her fault.

Part of his recent attitude could be attributed to his age. She well recalled being a sassy-mouthed teen who was constantly in trouble. Unlike Shane, who had someone who cared about him, wanted him to do well in life, Sage had no one to talk to or rely on.

The gloomy weather and her equally dark thoughts caused her to take a cleansing breath as she pulled into the parking lot at the deli. She hurried inside and paid for Matilda's order then accepted the offer of the college-aged kid to help carry everything out to her car. He set a box of individual Styrofoam containers full of steaming soup on the seat next to her while she placed two bags packed with sandwiches and chips on the floor.

"Thanks, Tyson," she said, smiling at the young man. He nodded then jogged back inside the warmth of the deli.

The fragrant scent of spices blended with the smell of melted cheese, filling her car with a mouth-watering aroma that made her stomach growl.

Matilda and Ruth had good taste, at least in food. The deli's tomato soup was the best she'd ever eaten. They roasted the tomatoes before processing them for the soup then added fresh basil and rich cream. If her taste buds hadn't deceived her, she thought there might be a bit of garlic in the soup. The cheese sandwiches were amazing, too. Three different cheeses were encased in sourdough bread then slathered in butter and grilled.

Sage could hardly wait to get home to share the soup and sandwiches with Shane. Happy to have one less thing to do that evening, she cranked up the radio and sang along to one of her favorite tunes. She was only two blocks from Golden Skies when she drove through an intersection and looked up to see someone run the stop sign and head straight for her.

It was too late to swerve, slam on the brakes, or speed out of the way. The smell of burning rubber blended with the acrid odor of her fear as the pickup slammed into her passenger door. The sound of squealing brakes, creaking metal, and shattering glass was the last thing Sage heard before she passed out.

Chapter Three

Justin pulled away from the drive-through window at the best hamburger joint in town and fished in the paper bag he'd just placed on the seat beside him. After snagging a hot, crispy French fry and popping it in his mouth, he pulled out a double bacon cheeseburger. Quickly folding down the paper wrapper, he bit into the burger then scrambled for a napkin to catch the greasy juice that threatened to dribble down his hand and across his chin. His dad always said the juicier the burger, the better it tasted. Justin had to agree as he took another big bite from the beef-filled house-made bun.

The town of Holiday boasted a pizza place, the deli, a diner, and the hamburger joint. There was The Blue, a bar that offered Buffalo wings, fries, and tacos. When people wanted to dress up and sit at a table that didn't come with a paper placemat or laminated menu they went to the Italian restaurant located not far from Golden Skies.

Right now, Justin was grateful for the burger place. He'd worked through lunch and breakfast had worn off long ago. In between bites of the burger and swiping at the juice, he dipped the double-battered fries into a disposable cup of ketchup he'd set on his console.

He'd just shoved two fries in his mouth as he neared an intersection and watched a pickup barrel right through the stop sign. In the beam from his headlights, he saw the teen driver look up as she broadsided the car in front of him, sending it skidding across the intersection. He slammed on the brakes and stared in horror as blood splashed seemingly everywhere inside the car the teen had struck. Thick red liquid dripped down the windows, like a macabre scene from a slasher movie.

Justin parked on the edge of the street, switched on his hazard lights, then jumped out of his pickup and dialed 9-1-1 as he ran toward the wreck.

When the operator answered, Justin gave her the basic details. "I just witnessed a two-car collision at the intersection of Main and Park. The driver of a pickup ran the stop sign and hit a car in the intersection."

"Help is being dispatched, sir. Please stay on the line."

"I will." Justin watched a teen girl climb out of the pickup, blubbering to someone on her cell phone. If he had to guess, he'd say texting while she was driving was probably the reason for the wreck in the first place.

"The driver of the pickup is out of the vehicle. The driver of the car has not exited," he said into the phone.

"Thank you for that information, sir. What is your name, sir?"

"Justin James."

"Thank you, sir. Please continue to stay on the line."

"Okay," he said, then rushed over to the teen. "Are you hurt?" he asked, noticing the pickup's front bumper absorbed most of the damage, at least from what he could see.

The teen shook her head so he ran around the smashed car to the driver's side door. Afraid of what he'd find inside, he could see the air bags had deployed, even if they were dripping with blood.

Quickly inhaling a deep breath, he pulled on the handle, but the door remained locked. Between the darkness of evening, airbags, rain, and blood, he couldn't see the driver.

"Hey, can you hear me?" he yelled close to the window. "Can you unlock the door?" He had no idea if the driver was alive, injured, dazed, or incoherent. He tapped on the glass. "Please, unlock the door."

Sirens blared in the distance. "Emergency response is on their way, sir," the 9-1-1 operator said in his ear. Justin had nearly forgotten he was still on the line with the operator until she spoke.

"I hear them coming," he said, then tapped on the window again. "The car appears to be full of blood, the doors are locked, and the driver seems unresponsive."

"Do you have a visual on the driver, sir?"

"No, the airbags, rain, dark, and blood are making it impossible to see inside." Justin was tempted to kick out the back window to check on the driver, but didn't want to do anything that might cause more harm to the person in the driver's seat. The car looked totaled, at least from the way the entire passenger side was caved in. What if there were passengers in the car? Kids?

His stomach churned at the thought of little ones being involved in the wreck. He glanced over at the teen driver who'd caused the accident. She was sitting on the ground, holding her head in one hand and the phone in the other as she continued to cry.

He started to walk over to offer her a word of comfort when a hand pressed against the driver's window, smearing the blood.

Startled, he jumped back then realized a hand moving around was a good sign. "It's okay. The ambulance is on its way," he said in a loud voice as he moved closer to the window. The smaller size of the hand and delicately long fingers made him think the driver had to be a woman. "Can you unlock the door?"

"No," he heard a choked voice say. "It's stuck."

"Don't worry. Help will be here soon." He placed his hand on the window, wondering if the driver could see it. The sound of sirens grew louder and a flash of color down the street announced the arrival of the emergency response team.

Justin stepped back and made his way over to where the teen struggled to get to her feet. He gave her a hand. "It's okay. We all make mistakes sometimes."

"I was texting my boyfriend and I know I'm not supposed to use my phone while I drive. It's his pickup and he's going to kill me," the teen said in such a rapid rush Justin had to strain to keep up with her words.

A police officer approached them as the rain gradually stopped. "I have some questions for you folks," the man said, opening his notebook while a crew worked to open the door of the wrecked car. Justin kept one eye on the police officer as he grilled the teen and the other on the team trying to open the car door. While they waited for the driver to be extracted, the paramedics looked over the teen. They declared her shaken up, but not injured.

"Are you a witness, sir?" the police officer asked Justin.

"Yes, sir. I was behind that car," Justin pointed to the wrecked sedan. "I saw the pickup run the stop sign and plow right into it."

"I didn't mean to." The teen's makeup ran in blue and black streaks down her cheeks as she continued to cry. One of the paramedics handed her a tissue before jogging over to the car. "I'm so sorry."

Justin took a step toward the car when the emergency response team lifted out a blood-covered woman. The scent of garlic filled the air and a frown wrinkled his brow. Was she some sort of vampire wanna-be?

The police officer had his hands full, trying to keep the teen from flying apart, but he looked at the smashed car and sniffed. "Smells like the tomato soup from the deli."

The air did carry the aroma of tomato soup. Justin walked over to where the woman they removed from the car rested on a stretcher while paramedics asked her questions and wiped her face.

"That's not blood, is it?" Justin asked.

"Tomato soup." A paramedic grabbed another towel to mop more soup off the woman's face. When he did, Justin sucked in a gasp.

"Sage?" he asked, shocked to see the beautiful receptionist from Golden Skies.

"Mr. James?" she asked, staring at him with dazed eyes.

"That's right. I'm glad you're going to be okay. You had me worried for a minute." Relief flooded over him. Although she appeared shaken up, the fact Sage was talking to him made him hopeful whatever injuries she sustained were minor. "Is there anyone I can call for you? Anything I can do?"

"The soup... Golden Skies... Matilda Dale," she said, closing her eyes and clenching her jaw.

"You were getting soup for Mrs. Dale? Is that what you're trying to say?"

"Yes," she whispered, not opening her eyes.

"I'll take care of it. Anyone else you want me to call. Your husband? Son?"

"Call Shane. Phone in purse," she said before she swallowed hard and clamped her mouth shut.

Justin bent down and glanced inside the car. The aroma of tomato soup laden with garlic and herbs blended with the scent of toasted cheese and the lingering smoky chemical odor caused by the air bags deploying. Tomato soup dripped off everything, covering every surface. No wonder he thought the car was full of blood.

He spied Sage's purse scrunched up against the center console. She was lucky the teen hadn't been going any faster or the wreck might have been far, far worse.

Heedless to the mess it would make on his clothes, he reached in with both hands and worked her purse free then carried it over to the stretcher.

"Phone?" Sage asked when he set the purse down beside her.

"Mind if I look for it?" he asked.

"No," she whispered, as though it hurt to talk.

Justin had been in one car wreck when he was five, but he didn't remember much about it other than the sound of squealing brakes and the jolt of the impact. Fortunately, he and his sister were safely buckled into the backseat and weren't hurt at all, other than a few cuts from the windshield breaking.

He felt like he was invading Sage's privacy as he opened her purse and looked for her phone, he checked a side pocket and found a tube of lip gloss. Another side pocket turned up a package of gum and roll of breath mints. He delved deeper into the bag, expecting the mess he imagined existed in most women's purses. Instead, he found an organizer with a variety of pockets and slots. It appeared Sage Presley liked things orderly and neat. He found her phone in a tall slot and pulled it out.

"Shane," she whispered. "Call Shane."

Justin assumed Shane was her husband. He held the phone out to her, but the paramedic shook his head. "She's not in any condition to talk right now. Do you know her? Can you call her family?"

"I know who she is and will make the call. Are you taking her to the hospital?"

"Yes. With all this soup covering her, it's hard to gauge the full extent of her injuries." The second paramedic said as they wheeled the stretcher to the ambulance and loaded it.

"Call Shane!" Sage said, sounding desperate.

"I will, Sage. I'll call and bring your phone to you at the hospital."

"Shane!" she yelled once before the paramedics closed the ambulance doors.

Justin answered a few more questions for the police officer, completing his statement about the accident, then he climbed in his pickup and turned on the overhead light. He tapped a button on Sage's phone and a screen opened to enter a password. With no idea what it could be, he typed in Shane. Surprisingly, the phone unlocked. He went to her recent calls and tapped one from Shane.

The phone rang three times before the squeaky sound of a boy in the midst of a voice change answered. "Before you start riding my case, I finished my homework and even put a load of laundry in the washer. Are you on your way home? I'm starving."

"Is this Shane?" Justin asked.

"Yeah, who's this? Where's Sage?" the boy's voice sounded uncertain, hesitant.

"My name is Justin. I've been working with

Sage at Golden Skies. She was in an accident and asked me to call you to let you know. Do you have someone there who can take you to the hospital?"

"No," the boy's voice came out choked. "Is she... is she gonna be okay?"

"I don't know, but I think so. Can you get to the hospital or do you need a ride?"

"I can walk," the boy said, then sniffled. "It's not that far from our house. Where should I go when I get there?"

"Go to the desk in the emergency room. They can tell you more there." Justin hated the kid was by himself. "I'll be there soon."

"Thanks," Shane said, sounding somewhat relieved. "Bye."

Justin disconnected the call then drove to Golden Skies. He'd barely set foot inside when Matilda Dale, her sweet friend Ruth, an older gent named Rand, and a handful of others shuffled out of the gathering room into the lobby.

"Justin!" Matilda said, bustling toward him. Before she reached out to squeeze his arm, she stopped and glared at him. "Why are you wearing tomato soup? You haven't seen Sage have you? She was supposed to be back ages ago with our soup and sandwiches."

"She was in an accident and can't bring your dinner. In fact, your soup is smeared all over the inside of her car."

"Oh, gracious!" Ruth said, her hand fluttering to her throat. "Is she injured? What can we do?"

"They took her to the hospital and I called Shane, but that's about all I know. She was talking and able to move so that's all good. I'm gonna go check on her, but she wanted me to let you know about dinner."

"Who cares about soup at a time like this? I'll call Fynlee. She'll want to know," Matilda said, spinning around and marching down the hall.

"Will you really go check on her?" Ruth asked, placing a gentle hand on Justin's arm, apparently unconcerned about the soup smeared all over the sleeve of his coat.

"I will. I told Shane I'd meet him there." Justin had a hundred questions he wanted to ask about Sage, her husband, and son, but now wasn't the time. "Do you need me to bring you dinner? Will you all be okay?"

"We will be fine. If I know my nephew and his bride, Fynlee and Carson will be at the hospital as soon as they can get there. She'll let us know how Sage is doing." Ruth smiled at him. "Thank you for coming to tell us." She turned to Matilda and Rand. "I suggest we all go to the cafeteria for dinner."

"That's probably a good idea," Justin said. He tipped his head to the older folks then hurried back out to his pickup.

He drove to the hospital and found a parking space in the far reaches of the lot. After tucking Sage's phone into his pocket, he turned up his coat collar against the cold evening air and covered the distance to the emergency entry in long strides.

When he stepped inside, he recognized a boy from seeing him with Sage. The teen stood at the nurse's station asking questions. He could see the boy had Sage's golden hair and they shared the same shape of face. There was no doubt in his mind they were related.

"Are you Shane?" Justin asked, stepping up to the boy and holding out his hand in greeting.

"Yes. Are you Justin?" the boy asked, taking the hand he'd extended and shaking it.

For a young teen, Shane had a strong grip. In fact, the boy had grown a few inches from the first time Justin had seen him with Sage and appeared to be filling out shoulders that would someday be broad.

"Are you related to Sage Presley?" the nurse asked, giving him a probing look.

"No. I was first to arrive at the scene of the accident and I have her cell phone. I promised her I'd return it." Justin took her phone from his pocket and handed it to Shane. "Is she going to be okay?"

"The doctor is running tests right now. If you aren't family, I can't tell you anything." The nurse glanced from him to Shane. "You can sit and wait over there." She pointed to a waiting room. "When the doctor has something to share, he'll find you."

Shane looked like he inwardly debated what would happen if he ran down the hallway and found Sage, so Justin tipped his head toward the waiting area. "Mind if I wait with you for a while?"

The boy shrugged. "I guess not."

Together, they took seats against the wall and waited. The tension lingering in the room was so thick he could practically see it as others awaited news of loved ones and friends. He leaned back and blew out a long breath before glancing over at Shane. "Is your dad coming?"

The boy's eyes widened and he shook his head. "No."

"Is he out of town?"

Shane offered him a strange look. "Yeah, he is."

"Mrs. Dale at Golden Skies mentioned Fynlee. Is she friends with Sage?"

Shane nodded. "They've been friends for quite a while. Fynlee just married Carson Ford a few weeks ago. His aunt, Ruth, and Miss Matilda are best friends." He leaned a little closer to Justin and dropped his voice. "Carson calls Golden Skies the Hokey Pokey Hotel."

Justin smirked. "That's a good name for it."

Shane almost smiled. "Yeah, it is."

Justin relaxed and removed his soup-smeared coat, setting it in the chair beside him. "So, what do you like to study in school?"

"The clock." Shane grinned. "That way I know when I can escape for the day."

"Not a fan of school, huh?"

Shane shook his head. "Not really."

"I bet a smart kid like you gets good grades, though."

Pride lifted Shane's shoulders and he nodded. "I do okay."

"Other than the clock, what else do you like to study?" Justin hoped to keep the boy talking and distracted until the doctor came to tell them how Sage was doing or someone else arrived to keep an eye on Shane.

"I like math and science classes best," the boy said, fiddling with Sage's phone as he held it in his hands. "My history teacher is okay, but my English teacher is a real…" Shane closed his mouth before he finished his statement.

"Loser?" Justin asked with a grin.

"Something like that," Shane agreed. He sat back in his chair and stopped toying with the cell phone. "How did you say you know Sage?"

Justin found it odd the boy called his mother by her first name, but didn't say anything. He still had trouble picturing her as old enough to have a son who was Shane's age. "I know her from Golden Skies."

"What do you do there?" Shane asked.

"I'm an electrician. Most of my time is spent in the new wing being added on to the facility. I've done a few small jobs for some of the residents, though."

"Like what?" Shane leaned forward, appearing interested in Justin's work.

"Installing new outlets. Between them all having cell phones, tablets, computers, and whatnot, they never have enough outlets." Justin grinned and felt the tense muscles of his shoulders relax. "And I think they just like the company."

"Yeah, they do." Shane sighed. "Sometimes, when I'm there waiting for Sage, I worry they'll talk my ears off, but they're nice. Mrs. Beaumont bakes the best cookies and pies."

Justin's eyebrows moved upward. "She does? That's good to know."

Shane studied him a moment. "You're not from around here, are you?"

Justin shook his head. "No. I moved here a

week before Thanksgiving. I was looking to start my own electrician business and when I heard there was one for sale here, I jumped at the opportunity to buy it."

In fact, Mr. Currin, who owned the Holiday Electric Company, had not only sold Justin the business, but also his house. The older man wanted to retire and move to Portland to be closer to his daughter and her family. Justin would have been an idiot to turn down his generous offer. It wasn't every day the opportunity to purchase an established company came along, especially when the deal included a well-maintained home with twenty acres of pasture. So far, Justin had no idea what he'd do with the property, but he liked that it was located on the edge of town. Mr. Currin had run his shop there, too. Justin found the arrangement convenient and continued it when he took over the business.

Truthfully, the three bedroom, two bath house was far more than he needed, but he hoped to someday settle down and raise a family. The house would be perfect then and the acreage would give kids a great place to play.

He could almost see brown-haired, green-eyed little ones running through the pasture, chasing a floppy-eared dog.

Why those children appeared green-eyed left him slightly disturbed, considering the boy sitting across from him had green eyes that were the exact shade as his mother's intriguing eyes.

Justin began to wonder if Mr. Presley was in the picture. Perhaps Sage was divorced. Maybe there was still hope to win her heart. But if she had a son in the eighth grade, just how old was she? And how in the world did she appear so young and innocent?

Even covered head to toe in tomato soup, she looked beautiful.

Chagrined by the direction of his thoughts, especially toward another man's wife, Justin did his best to shift his thoughts back to Shane. "Do you play sports?"

"Not right now. I played football, but I'm not into the winter sports. I might play baseball, though." Shane's stomach growled and he tossed Justin a sheepish grin.

"Sounds like you're hungry. Want to go with me to the cafeteria? My dinner got abruptly interrupted, so I could use something, too."

"Sure." Shane stood and followed Justin out of the waiting room.

They stopped at the nurse's station to tell her they were going to the cafeteria in case the doctor or anyone else came looking for them. Once they looked over the selections in the cafeteria, Justin and Shane both tried the rotisserie-style chicken. Shane had macaroni and cheese with his while Justin ordered rice and broccoli.

After they finished eating, they returned to the waiting room as a couple raced inside.

"Shane! Are you okay, honey?" Fynlee Ford asked as she wrapped the boy in a hug. Justin admired the warmth and friendliness that fairly oozed from her. The woman was tall, lovely, and glowing with the happiness only a newlywed can possess.

"I'm fine," Shane said, pulling back from her and ducking his head, although Justin noted his pleased smile.

Fynlee looked to Justin. "Grams told me you were at the accident scene and were coming here. Thank you for sitting with Shane. I'm sure Sage appreciates it, even if she doesn't necessarily know it yet." She glanced over her shoulder at a brawny cowboy standing behind her. "Oh, I'm sorry. Carson, this is Justin James. He's the electrician doing all the work in the new wing at Golden Skies."

"Carson Ford," the man said, reaching out to shake his hand. "Nice to meet you."

"You as well, Carson. You bought Mrs. Beaumont's ranch?"

"Yep. Aunt Ruth sold it to me after Uncle Bob passed away. I love it here." Carson wrapped his hands around Fynlee's waist and pulled her back against him before kissing her cheek. "If I hadn't taken over the ranch, I would never have fallen head over heels for this girl."

"That's a great reason to be happy in Holiday," Justin said, amazed by the love shining from Carson's and Fynlee's faces as they looked at each other.

Fynlee turned her attention back to Shane. "Did you get dinner? Do you want me to take you to get something to eat?"

"Justin and me went to the cafeteria and had chicken. It was pretty good," Shane said, then turned to Justin. "Thank you for buying my dinner.

I didn't bring my wallet, but I can pay you back."

"Don't worry about it. My treat," Justin said, smiling at Shane. He knew with Carson and Fynlee there, he should leave, but he was hesitant to go until he found out how Sage was doing.

"How's the project at work coming along?" Fynlee asked, motioning to a group of empty chairs in the waiting room.

Glad to have a reason to linger, Justin sat down next to Shane, across from Fynlee and Carson. "It's going well and so far it's staying on track. We should have it finished and ready to open by the end of April."

"That's wonderful. The extra care the facility will be able to offer because of that wing is much needed in the community. I heard the other day they already have a waiting list for the rooms." Fynlee gave him an odd, questioning glance. "You haven't had any unwanted visitors while you're working, have you?"

Justin grinned. "A few of the residents have stuck their heads in to see what's going on, but for the most part they've stayed away. Your grandmother is Mrs. Dale?"

"That's right." Fynlee smiled. "I should probably apologize for whatever inappropriate thing she has said or done, because I'm sure there has been at least one circumstance since you've been working there."

Justin chuckled. "Oh, nothing too bad, other than she seems to like to squeeze my arms a lot."

Carson snorted. "She used to do that to me, too. Matilda walks to her own ten-piece band. I'd say drummer, but it's far and above much more than that."

"So I noticed," Justin grinned again. "But she means well. I still have a hard time figuring out how she and your aunt are such good friends since they are nothing alike."

"They balance each other," Fynlee said with a soft smile. "Ruth would be too reserved and Grams too crazy if they didn't have one another to rely on."

"It's nice they're such good friends. Do you…" Justin shut his mouth and rose to his feet as a doctor walked into the room.

"Family of Sage Presley?" the man asked.

"That's us," Fynlee said, settling her hands on Shane's shoulders.

"Sage is one lucky young woman. Other than a slight concussion and a few cuts and bruises, she'll be just fine. She needs a day or two to rest, but since tomorrow's Friday, I think she should be able to get back to her normal activities on Monday. I expect she'll be really sore tomorrow and have a headache, but beyond that, she'll be back to herself soon enough."

Shane took a shuddering breath, as though he tried to hold back his tears, while Fynlee gave his shoulders a hug.

"Hear that, kiddo? She'll be fine." Fynlee kissed his cheek then looked to the doctor again. "Will you keep her overnight or should we take her home?"

"She can go home if someone will keep an eye on her. You don't need to wake her up frequently, but just check in on her once or twice during the night. The best thing to help her heal is sleep," the doctor said.

"We'll take her home with us," Carson said, stepping closer to Fynlee. "She can stay at the ranch this weekend and we can keep an eye on her."

"I'll go sign Sage's release papers and tell the nurse to get her ready to go," the doctor said, then left the room.

"I don't know if she'll like that, going to the ranch, I mean," Shane said, obviously concerned about doing what was best for Sage.

"You'll stay with us, too, of course," Fynlee said, giving Shane another hug. "Why don't we go to your house? You can get whatever you and Sage will need for the weekend then we can come back and take you both home with us. How does that sound?"

"Good," Shane said, visibly relieved.

"Is there anything I can do to help?" Justin asked, not sure what he could do, but wanting to offer his assistance if it was needed.

"I think we've got this, but thank you for everything," Fynlee said, offering him another warm smile. "We'll take it from here."

Justin wanted to see Sage, to make sure she was fine for himself, but he had no reason to be there. He placed a hand on Shane's shoulder and gave it a slight squeeze. "You take care of yourself and Sage."

"I will, and thanks, Justin, for dinner and for… everything."

"You're welcome." Justin tipped his head to

Fynlee then walked toward the doorway before glancing back. "I'll see you around."

He stepped outside into a bone-chilling rain that had started falling again. As he made his way to his pickup, he couldn't help but wonder why, of all the women in the town of Holiday, the one he couldn't seem to chase out of his head had to be already taken.

Chapter Four

Sage awoke with her thoughts enshrouded in a fog while pain knifed through her head. She licked dry lips and tried to think of what she'd done to make her body so sore and achy. The deep breath she inhaled filled her nose with the smell of something smoky, like burnt chemicals, along with garlic.

A groan rolled out of her as she recalled going to get soup and sandwiches at the deli before someone hit her car.

One minute she'd been singing along to a song on the radio and looking forward to going home to a meal she didn't have to cook. The next moment, she was about to drown in exploded containers of tomato soup with the airbag in her face.

She remembered looking to her right at bright headlights heading straight toward her then the impact when the pickup hit her passenger side. A blank in her memory made her think she must have passed out at one point. A man was there. He promised to call Shane.

Thoughts of her brother made her eyes snap open and she looked around. Her gaze roved over the antique maple bedroom set, pale yellow walls, and sunlight filtering in the window. At least it had stopped raining.

Sage forced herself to sit up and grasped her head in her hands, hoping to stop the pounding that was joined by a wave of dizziness. She closed her eyes then slowly opened them again. The room was unfamiliar, but outside the window she could see cattle in a pasture.

Vague memories of Carson and Fynlee bringing her and Shane to the ranch surfaced. She must still be at the Flying B. At least she hoped that's where she was. If it was, she knew her friends would take good care of Shane. She sent up a prayer of thanks he hadn't been in the car with her. If he had…

A wave of nausea rolled over her as Sage considered how badly Shane could have been injured. She took another deep breath, inhaling that same, horrible smell that made her want to gag. Two hard swallows only served to amplify her need of a drink of water. She gauged the distance to the door when it suddenly swung open.

"Good morning, darling," Matilda said as she and Ruth walked inside the room. Matilda held a stack of books and magazines while Ruth carried a tray.

Sage scooted back against the headboard then Ruth set the tray on her lap. A glass of water, a cup of steaming, fragrant tea, two pieces of toast and a scrambled egg all looked appealing. "Where am I? Where's Shane?" she asked as she lifted the glass of water and took a deep drink.

"At the Flying B. Carson dropped Shane off at school then brought us out to spend the day with you since Fynlee has to work." Ruth placed the back of her hand against Sage's forehead. "No fever. Does your head hurt?"

"Some," Sage said, unwilling to admit to the two old dears how badly her head ached.

"Eat your breakfast and drink your tea. It will make you feel better," Matilda said, setting the books and magazines on the nightstand. "You might want something to read later, when you feel better."

"Today is Friday?" Sage asked, trying to gain a firmer hold on her bearings.

"That's right. You were bringing back our soup and sandwiches last night when a pickup ran a stop sign and hit your car." Ruth patted Sage on the shoulder. "I don't think much can be done to save your car, honey. It's a wonder you made it out of the wreck with nothing more than a concussion and a few cuts and bruises."

A concussion would explain the pain in her head as well as the dizziness and her overall disoriented feeling.

"We are so sorry, darling. If we hadn't asked you to pick up our dinner, none of this would have happened." Matilda squeezed her hand.

"No, it wasn't your fault. And I truly didn't

mind running the errand for you." Sage released a sigh. "I just don't know what I'll do without a car."

"Do you have insurance?" Ruth asked.

"I do, but my car was older. I'm sure it won't be worth much." Sage took a sip of the sweet tea. A whiff of ginger penetrated the nasty odor stuck in her nose and made her relax slightly.

"I've got a car I haven't driven for a while and it's parked in the garage here. You might as well use it," Ruth offered.

"Oh, Ruth, that's so sweet, but I wouldn't want to impose." Sage wondered what kind of car she'd be able to buy with the small amount she was sure the insurance office would offer her. Even though the accident wasn't her fault, she doubted she'd end up with more than a few hundred dollars for her car.

"I insist, Sage. That car isn't doing anyone any good just taking up space in the garage. You might as well drive it." Ruth gave her a kind smile. "Now, we are here to take care of you today. If you need anything, all you have to do is let us know."

"That's so kind of you, and of Carson and Fynlee, but I should go home. You all have better things to do than wait on me hand and foot. I'm sure I'll be fine after this lovely breakfast."

Matilda shook her head, making the red chandelier earrings she wore chime and tinkle like miniature bells. "The doctor told Fynlee you need to spend the weekend resting if you want to go back to work on Monday. You are staying here for the weekend and so are we. Fynlee will bring Shane home from school when she gets off work. That boy is quite excited about the prospect of staying here until Sunday afternoon. You wouldn't want to disappoint him."

"No, I wouldn't," Sage said, aware Matilda had just cleverly maneuvered her into doing what she wanted by leveraging Shane. In truth, Sage was grateful she wouldn't have to deal with anything for a day or two. With the way she currently felt, she knew it was smart to rest and heal.

She glanced up at Matilda, taking in the woman's white blouse with black polka dots and black pants with white polka dots along with a pair of bright red shoes and a chunky red beaded necklace. For Matilda, it was a rather tame outfit. As usual, Ruth looked like the epitome of someone's doting grandmother with her soft pink sweater over a muted floral dress.

"Are you two stuck babysitting me today?" she asked with a smile, wondering how bad it could be to be doted on by Ruth and Matilda for the day. It would most likely be fun for them to have someone to fuss over.

"We are and you have to listen to everything we say," Matilda said with a cheeky grin. "My first command is for you to spill the beans about how well you know Justin James."

"Justin James?" Sage took another sip from her tea, curious why Matilda would ask that. She hadn't told anyone, not even Fynlee, about her interest in the electrician. There wasn't any point in it. Not when she had no plans to date anyone. The entire focus of her world was on raising her brother and whatever it took to make sure he was fed, clothed, and taken care of. A relationship with a hunky, handsome, ruggedly masculine man was the last thing she needed to consider.

"Don't you remember, honey? He arrived on the scene first, called 9-1-1, and stayed with you until help arrived," Ruth said, relaying the details she knew. "He rescued your purse from the car and you asked him to call Shane. Fynlee said he waited at the hospital with Shane until she and Carson could get there. He even made sure Shane had dinner."

"He did?" Sage was taken aback by that tidbit of news. She gained clarity and realized he was the man she recalled helping her. For some reason, she hadn't made the connection until Ruth said he'd been there. "That was so kind of him."

"Kind my sweet patootie. I think that boy likes you," Matilda said in her typically blunt fashion.

Sage blushed and hid behind the cup of tea.

"I do think you've caught his eye," Ruth said with a tender smile. "He seems like a very nice boy."

Sage wanted to laugh at the way Matilda and Ruth referred to Justin as a boy. She assumed he had to be in his late twenties. Not only that, but he was successful enough in his career to become a master electrician and purchase his own business before the age of thirty. That said something about him, about his character and drive. If she was interested in dating, Justin would have been a great guy to get to know.

However, that just wasn't meant to be and wishing wouldn't change the fact she had a teenager to raise and the accompanying responsibilities to handle. Shane would always have to come first.

Suddenly tired, Sage set the nearly empty cup of tea on the tray and fought against the heaviness of her eyelids.

"You rest for now, Sage. We'll check on you in a little while," Ruth said, lifting the tray off her lap.

"If you need anything, call the house phone. We left your cell phone right there on the nightstand where you could reach it." Matilda pointed to the phone that was sitting next to the stack of reading material.

"Thank you," Sage whispered, before drifting off to sleep.

That evening, after she'd dressed in one of the outfits Fynlee had packed for her, she sat in the living room with Ruth, Matilda, and Fynlee when Shane raced inside.

"Guess what, Sage?" His eyes danced with life as he rushed over to where she sat in a recliner with her feet up and head resting against the back.

"I'll never guess, so just tell me," she said, thrilled to see her brother so excited.

"Carson let me watch as a mama cow had babies. She had twins, a bull calf and a..." He appeared to search his thoughts, trying to remember the proper term to use.

"Heifer?" Fynlee asked.

"Yeah, that's it," Shane said, with a broad smile. "I took a photo of them so you could see, too."

Shane handed his phone to Sage and she scrolled through the photos he'd taken of the two newborn calves. "Oh, they are adorable." She gave his phone back to him. Sage wasn't sure she was comfortable with him observing the process of giving birth, even if it was with livestock. However, at thirteen, she supposed it was time for her to realize Shane was no longer a little boy and many strange, uncomfortable conversations loomed in her future.

"I'm gonna go back out to see them." Shane shoved his phone into his pocket and hurried toward the door.

"Keep your jacket zipped and cover up your ears," she called after him.

Shane glanced back at her and rolled his eyes then rushed outside and closed the door.

Matilda and Ruth chuckled. "You've got this mothering thing down pat, Sage. How long have you been taking care of Shane?"

"Since I turned eighteen," she said, smiling at the two older women. "Raising him is my privilege." Sage wouldn't trade the time she'd spent with her brother for anything. In a few short years, he'd be out on his own and she could reevaluate what she wanted to do with the rest of her life then. Until he left to make his own way in the world, nothing else mattered but Shane.

Occasionally, Sage dreamed of a knight in shining armor riding to her rescue and relieving her of the burden of responsibility that so often weighed her down. The handsome but mysterious man always carried a big bouquet of daisies and spoke in a soft, husky tone that made her wish he was real.

Then she'd take a breath, bring herself back to reality, and be grateful she had Shane in her life.

The next morning when she awakened, her head barely ached, the dizziness had dissipated, but her body felt stiff and sore. She had a bruise across her stomach from the seatbelt and her neck hurt, but she knew that was to be expected.

She showered and dressed then followed the scents of coffee and bacon downstairs. Thankful the nasty odors that had lingered in her nose disappeared overnight, she took a deep breath of the delicious aromas of breakfast.

When she stepped into the kitchen, she found Ruth busy flipping pancakes while Matilda set the table and Fynlee poured orange juice in glasses.

"Good morning, darling," Matilda said, hurrying over to give her an exuberant hug.

Sage hid a wince when Matilda tightened her arms around her, causing her sore ribs to protest, then kissed her cheek.

"Good morning," Sage said, glancing around the kitchen. "What can I do to help?"

"Just sit yourself down at the table. Everything will be ready in a minute. Shane and Carson are on their way in," Fynlee said. She gave her a studying glance as she finished pouring the juice. "You look like you feel better today."

"I do feel better." Sage carried four juice glasses over to the table and set them down, then smiled at her friend. "I can't thank you all enough for taking care of us this weekend. I don't know what I would have done if you hadn't been so kind."

Fynlee placed her hands on Sage's shoulders and gave her a gentle squeeze. "That's what friends are for, Sage. We're happy to help. Besides, Carson said Shane is having a great time hanging out with the guys. He got to see another baby born this morning."

"I'm sure he'll be excited to tell us all about it." Sage looked up as Carson and Shane entered through the back door and removed their coats and boots. She had no idea where Shane had acquired the old pair of cowboy boots he wore, but could only surmise Carson had provided them. She just hoped Shane knew the fun he was having at the ranch was a one-time experience, not something they'd do with any frequency.

After breakfast, Sage insisted on helping with the dishes while Shane followed Carson back outside. She found herself exhausted before the last dish was loaded in the dishwasher and barely made it upstairs to her room before she collapsed on the bed and slept until noon.

Streaks of indigo and crimson filled the sky when she made her way to the kitchen following another nap that afternoon. Ruth stirred a pan of gravy while Matilda mashed potatoes and Fynlee assembled a green salad.

"Oh, your cheeks look rosy again," Matilda said with a smile when she walked into the room.

"Is that a good thing?" Sage asked with a teasing grin.

"A very good thing, darling," Matilda said, kissing her cheek then returning her focus to the potatoes.

"May I help with anything?"

Fynlee nodded to a stack of plates on the

counter. "If you wouldn't mind setting the table that would be appreciated."

"I think I can handle that," Sage said, picking up the plates and placing them on the table.

When Shane and Carson came in to wash up for dinner, Sage thought her brother's feet might be floating a few inches above the floor. She'd never seen him so happy and enthusiastic before.

Shane was a good kid, but he'd gone through a lot in his short lifetime. Sometimes, he could be withdrawn and sullen. To see him having such a good time filled her heart to overflowing. Perhaps the wreck was worth it just to give him a memorable weekend.

"How are the twins?" Ruth asked as Shane and Carson stepped into the kitchen.

Carson wrapped his arms around Fynlee and kissed her neck. She turned and gave him a private smile. Sage was reminded that the two of them had been married less than a month, and here they were with four extra guests they hadn't planned on for the weekend.

She would definitely get out of their hair tomorrow. In fact, there was no reason she couldn't take Ruth and Matilda home after church so Carson and Fynlee could have the rest of the day together.

"The twins are so cute, but their mom is being a pain," Shane said, coming to stand next to Sage as she set napkins at each place setting.

"What's wrong?" Fynlee asked, glancing at Carson.

"The mama refuses to allow the bull calf to eat. We're gonna have to bottle feed him." Carson looked over at Shane. "Shane did a good job feeding him this morning and this evening."

"You got to feed the baby?" Sage asked, impressed. "Was it fun?"

"Yeah, it was. Fred acts like he's starving to death." Shane grinned. "He flicks his tail back and forth while he eats."

"Fred? Is that what you named him?" Sage asked, looking from Shane to Carson.

"I told him he could name the calf if he fed it," Carson said, grinning at Sage.

"Fred Asteer," Matilda said, clapping her hands together with glee. "That's what we'll call him. And his sister can be Ginger."

"That's a fun idea, Tilly," Ruth said, pouring the gravy into a serving bowl. "I always loved to watch Fred and Ginger dance across the silver screen."

Shane's brows knit together in confusion as he stared from Ruth to Matilda. "Who are Fred and Ginger?"

"Only two of the best dancers who ever tapped their way across a stage," Matilda said, executing a few dance steps followed by a spin and flourish of her arms.

Sage grinned and applauded while Matilda took a bow. "They were famous back in their day, Shane. Fred Astaire and Ginger Rogers played in many movies together. Maybe we can watch one sometime."

"I'm sure we can find one to watch this evening," Fynlee said, carrying the bowl of salad to the table. "If you're interested."

"Sure," Shane said with a shrug. He watched as Carson pulled out a chair for Fynlee and Ruth. The boy mimicked his actions and pulled out chairs for Matilda and Sage.

"Thank you, sweetheart," Matilda said, patting Shane on the back as he took a seat next to her.

Conversation throughout dinner was lively, carried mostly by Matilda and Ruth discussing the good old days and the rest of them asking just enough questions to keep them talking.

Sage and Fynlee did the dishes while Ruth and Matilda decided on which Fred Astaire movie they wanted to share with Shane. He went with Carson to finish a few chores then they all gathered in the living room with bowls of buttery popcorn to watch *Swing Time.*

The movie, from 1936, was one Sage was sure Shane would find boring, but the boy intently watched it, especially when Fred and Ginger danced. When the movie ended, he looked at Matilda and Ruth with a broad grin. "That was cool."

"We're glad you enjoyed it, darling," Matilda said, giving Shane a hug.

The following evening, Sage glanced at Shane as he helped her with the dinner dishes. "Do you have homework you need to finish?" she asked.

"Nope. I did it all on Friday. Carson said his mom always made them do their homework on Fridays, when they got home from school. That way, they could enjoy the rest of the weekend without dreading Sunday evening."

"That's a great way to do things," Sage said,

wondering why she hadn't thought of it herself. She'd always hated to do homework and put it off until the last possible second. Shane wasn't much better, but she was glad he took the advice and wisdom shared with him throughout the duration of the weekend to heart. In fact, she'd heard "Carson said" so many times, it made her work to hold back her giggles each time Shane mentioned something else he'd learned from the rancher.

"Do you think we could watch another old movie tonight?" Shane asked as he dried a pan and set it inside a cabinet.

"I think that would be fun." Sage smiled at her brother. "Want to watch another Fred and Ginger flick?"

"Yeah. Maybe I can pick up some dance moves for the spring dance." Shane grinned and pretended to tap dance a few steps.

"I'm sure if you wanted to learn to dance like that, Matilda and Ruth could help you."

Rather than look repulsed, Shane appeared interested. Despite her discomfort and loss of her car with the wreck, she was thankful Shane had a weekend to just be a carefree kid. Heaven only knew what good things might come from the weekend spent at the ranch.

Chapter Five

"Yoo-hoo!" Matilda Dale called as she stood in a doorway that led to the new wing and waved to Justin.

He looked over at her and wondered what she and Ruth Beaumont were up to now. He hadn't seen much of the women since the night of Sage's accident. That was three weeks ago. He'd been busy with work, but had made time to check on Sage a few times. He'd even offered to give her a ride if she ever needed it.

She told him Ruth decided she wanted to sell her car and had given her a good deal on it. Justin had gone out to the parking lot with Sage and admired the 1993 Cadillac. It looked as good as it must have the day it rolled off the showroom floor, and had less than fifty-thousand miles on it. Although the car had an outdated body style, Sage assured him the leather seats and luxurious interior made for a comfortable ride.

"I think she could have gotten five times as much for this car as she charged me, but I'm truly thankful for it," Sage had said as they walked back inside Golden Skies.

Justin had wanted to linger with Sage, but he hadn't. As far as he was concerned, the woman was off limits, even if her husband appeared to be a jerk. Maybe she was divorced. One of these days, he'd have to do a little investigating, but for now he needed to focus on finishing this job for Golden Skies. He only had a few weeks left to complete all the work with Matt's help.

Matilda's hand flapping at him with impatience drew him back to the present moment.

"Afternoon, Mrs. Dale, Mrs. Beaumont," Justin said as the woman insistently motioned him over. He bit back a grin at Matilda's colorful outfit. She wore a pair of black pants with bright pink flowers blooming up the legs, a canary-yellow striped shirt, and a lime green necklace that looked like heavy tire chains. "How may I assist you ladies?"

"We're sorry to bother you, Justin, knowing how busy you are, but we neglected to properly thank you for your help the evening of Sage's accident. You were most kind to come and let us know what had happened," Ruth said, offering him a warm smile. She put him in mind of his own grandmother who had passed away a few years back. He still missed her gentle presence and subtle wisdom in his life.

"I didn't do anything, other than tell you Sage

was in an accident and wouldn't bring your dinner. You already thanked me for that." He shrugged and looked at the two older women.

"You drove out of your way to tell us in person then offered to get us dinner if we needed it," Matilda stated in a matter-of-fact tone. "Besides, you went to the hospital and sat with Shane until Fynlee and Carson arrived. So thank you."

Matilda held out a bright purple gift bag with orange polka-dotted tissue paper stuffed inside.

Justin took the bag, removed the tissue, and pulled out a T-shirt. He unfolded it and held it up, unable to hide a grin. "I work with strippers" was emblazoned across the front along with a silhouette of a pair of wire strippers.

"This is great. Thank you so much," he said, smiling at the two women.

"Try it on! We want to see how it looks," Matilda said in an insistent tone.

Ruth placed a hand on Matilda's arm, as though she could restrain her friend's demands and ideas. "Now, Tilly, let's leave the boy alone and let him get back to work."

"Not just yet. It's only half as fun if he doesn't model the shirt for us," Matilda said, her vermilion-coated lips rolling into a pout.

Justin wondered how an octogenarian could appear so girlish, but Matilda Dale had it down to an art.

Rather than disappoint her, he unbuttoned his work shirt and slipped it off then pulled the T-shirt on over his head.

"How's it look?" he asked, wondering if

Matilda had purposely ordered a size too small or if it had been an accident. The shirt clung to every muscle and outlined every line and ridge of his form.

"Mmm. I'm not sure. Let's get another opinion." Matilda grabbed his hand and tugged him out of the construction area. He went along, not wanting to disrupt her fun. However, he hoped no one saw him parading around in the T-shirt that was outrageously tight.

Ruth strolled along on his other side. "We really should let him get back to work, Tilly."

"Oh, bosh. This will just take a moment." Matilda said, leading him down the hallway to the lobby.

Justin wanted to pull away and turn around when he saw Sage sitting at the receptionist's desk talking to someone on the telephone. She wore her hair twisted away from her face and secured at the back of her head in a tidy knot, although a few wisps escaped and danced around her cheeks. She looked lovely in a pink top that brought out roses in her cheeks and accented the soft shade of her lips. Lips that looked so inviting and entirely too kissable.

Annoyed with himself for noticing every detail about her appearance, he freed himself from Matilda's grasp. "I don't want to bother her. She's busy working and I should be, too."

"Fiddle-faddle," Matilda said, giving him a push forward. "See, she just hung up the phone."

Justin started to argue, but Matilda gave him another push and waved a hand at Sage. "Sage, darling, we need your opinion."

Sage glanced up from the note she was writing then did a double take. Her amazing green eyes widened in shock as she gaped at him. Slowly, amusement lifted the corners of her mouth into a smile.

"What kind of opinion, Matilda?" Sage asked, leaning back in her desk chair. Her gaze lifted and Justin felt the impact when it collided with his. Something magnetic and strong arced between them, like electricity dancing between two points of contact.

"We bought this shirt for Justin as a thank you for his help the night of your accident. What do you think? Does it fit him okay?" Matilda asked. The brazen old woman ran her hand across the width of his chest then had the audacity to wink at him.

Sage studied him for a long moment, her glance sweeping from his face and over his chest then back to meet his eyes. "I couldn't imagine it fitting any better," she said. Her cheeks flushed a dark shade of pink and she shifted her gaze to Ruth. "It was sweet of you two to buy him that shirt. Did you pick it out, Matilda?"

"I certainly did. The moment I saw it, Justin came to mind," Matilda said with pride in her voice.

Justin thought if she'd been a bird, she would have started preening her feathers.

"Well, you did good, Miss Matilda." Sage winked at her then at Ruth before looking back to Justin. "I don't think I've properly extended my thanks to you, Mr. James, for all you did to help me and Shane that evening. I truly am in your debt."

"No, you aren't. You've thanked me several times and it's nothing I wouldn't have done for anyone else in the same circumstances. I'm just glad you weren't seriously injured and things turned out the way they did." Justin was mindful of Sage's gaze lingering on his chest. Uncomfortable under the scrutiny, he took a step back. "Now, if you'll excuse me, I think I better get to work. Have a nice afternoon, ladies."

"Oh, we will, Justin. We certainly will." He felt three sets of eyes boring into his back as he hurried away from the desk and turned the corner into the hallway.

He glanced down at the ridiculous T-shirt and grinned. The guys would get a kick out of it, he was sure.

When he walked back to the construction area, he picked up his discarded shirt and the gift bag Matilda had left behind, carrying them over to where he'd left his tools.

"What are you wearing?" Matt asked as he turned around and stared at him.

"A gift from my girlfriends," Justin said. He returned to the outlet he'd been wiring before Ruth and Matilda arrived.

"Girlfriends?" Bull asked. "Weren't you just complaining a while back you couldn't find a woman to date and now you have more than one?"

Tim laughed and pointed to the T-shirt. "Anyone who lives here does not count as a girlfriend. I saw Mrs. Dale and her sidekick at the door earlier. That's quite a shirt."

Justin pulled the snug fabric away from his

chest. "Yes, it is. I wouldn't hurt their feelings for the world, though, so I'm wearing it until we finish up today. Get a good look, boys, because you might never see it again."

"I don't need an eyeful of what you've got on display," Joe said, waving a hammer in his direction. "Just because we're not all muscle-bound gym rats doesn't mean you need to rub our noses in it."

"I'm not rubbing your nose in anything, you idiot. For your information, I don't go to the gym. "

"That's right. You were just born that way," Joe said, grinning at him.

Justin swallowed down a stinging retort and took the good-natured ribbing as they finished their work for the afternoon.

Glad it was Friday, Justin looked forward to the weekend off. He'd been working fourteen-hour days the past two weeks and needed a break. He planned to get a pizza, head home, and do nothing all evening but relax. Tomorrow, he wanted to tackle the yard work he'd put off since he'd been so busy at Golden Skies and taking care of other electrical jobs that popped up.

With spring right around the corner, he needed to fertilize the lawn, clean out the flower beds around the house, and he'd noticed a section of sagging fence around the west side of the pasture. He still hadn't decided what to do with the pasture. He had almost eighteen acres of fenced grass and knew he could probably rent it, but wasn't sure that's what he wanted to do. Admittedly, he didn't have time to care for livestock of any kind.

He barely remembered to feed Crosby, the old cat Mr. Currin had left at the house with detailed instructions on the animal's preferred care.

Although the cat lived outside, it wanted to be fed in the garage. Cats roaming around the area would flock to the back porch if Crosby's food dish was outside, turning his dinner time into an all-you-can-eat buffet for felines.

Twice a day, Justin let the persnickety cat into the garage to eat. Sometimes the cat would stay on a bed in the garage for the evening. Other times, Crosby would yowl to get out five minutes after Justin let him in.

He felt sorry for Crosby, though. Mr. Currin said the cat would never adjust to a new place, especially since he'd lived at the same house since he was a kitten. From what he knew, Crosby had belonged to Mrs. Currin and when she passed away, the cat had never been quite the same. So Justin had agreed to take over his care.

Crosby was the most obstinate, paranoid, freakish cat he'd ever encountered, though. Although he seemed to be in good shape for his age, the cat appeared to be terrified of everything. Leaves blowing across the grass scared him. The sound of rain on the roof frightened him. A neighboring dog barking nearly sent him scrambling up Justin's leg in terror. He wasn't sure, but he thought he even saw the cat jump one day when he noticed his own shadow.

In spite of his multitude of fears, Crosby had many opinions about where and how he was fed. He refused to eat any of the treats or bites of meat

Justin offered to him. Crosby preferred the cheapest brand of cat food over more expensive varieties Justin had attempted to feed him.

Then there was the water bowl drama. Crosby wanted to drink directly from the faucet outside. During the winter, Justin had covered the faucet with insulation to keep it from freezing. Now that the weather was nicer, the cat would hover beneath the faucet, eagerly lapping water. If Justin didn't have time to indulge him, Crosby would stand with his two front feet in his water bowl and intermittingly paw at the water, presumably to aerate it. This resulted in Justin having to change the water twice a day because the cat considered it dirty after he played in it.

Most days, he didn't mind catering to the old feline's whims. However, when he arrived home that evening and the cat started yowling at the back door to come inside, Justin was half tempted to ignore him. Instead, he opened the door and picked up the cat, giving him several friendly rubs as he carried the mottled black and white feline to the garage.

Justin flicked on the light and glanced into Crosby's food bowl. He could have sworn it had food left in it that morning, but it was completely empty. Nary a crumb remained in the bowl.

"That's weird," he muttered as he put more food in the bowl. Crosby wanted the food to be fresh at each meal. The cat would actually nose around anything that was left behind unless he was truly hungry. Then he'd eat anything he could get his paws on.

"Were you starving this morning, buddy?" Justin asked as he gave the cat a good scratch on his back. "You do know you're spoiled, don't you, Crosby?"

The cat glanced up at him and blinked green eyes that made Justin think of Sage. Annoyed his mind kept circling back around to the beautiful woman, Justin had to get his wayward thoughts under control. After all, he had no idea if Sage was married, single, divorced, or in a relationship. And he still couldn't quite figure out how someone who seemed so young could have a teenage son.

Determined to relax and enjoy his evening, Justin went to the kitchen, washed his hands, then carried his pizza into the great room and sat in his big leather recliner. He ate pizza, mindlessly watched a movie, and fought the urge to close his eyes and rest.

After falling asleep in his chair at half past seven, he woke up with a stiff neck at ten and a furious cat yowling to be let out of the garage.

The next morning, he slept until eight, fed the cat, put a load of laundry in the washing machine then went outside to start his spring clean-up project. Mr. Currin assured him the flower beds required little care once they were cleaned in the spring. Justin looked forward to seeing the flowers that would soon shoot up and bloom.

He finished the flower beds, trimmed dead branches off a tree, and then fertilized the lawn. In a tool shed behind the house he found supplies to fix the fence. Crosby wandered out and kept brushing against his legs as he worked. Finally, Justin set aside the tools and picked up the cat, rubbing him behind his ears in a spot that always made him purr.

"What's the deal today, Crosby? Normally, you ignore me when I come outside."

The cat purred louder in response.

"You really are a crazy cat."

The cat swished his tail, whether in rebuttal or agreement Justin couldn't be sure.

He grinned and set the cat down then went back to work. By lunch time, he'd finished the project and could spend the afternoon doing something fun, or nothing at all.

Justin returned the fencing supplies to the shed then went inside the house. He ate leftover pizza for lunch while he went through a stack of mail and paid bills.

Rather than prop up his feet and indulge in a nap, he decided to clean his house. It was a good thing his mother insisted he learn basic housekeeping skills. No matter how much he hated to do it, the fact remained that he could. So he spent the next hour cleaning his bathroom, scrubbing sinks, and mopping the kitchen floor.

He'd just dropped another load of laundry in the washer when his phone rang. He closed the lid on the washer and stepped into the kitchen.

"Holiday Electric," he said, when he didn't recognize the number.

"Justin? This is Carson Ford. Is this a good time to catch you?"

Justin wondered why Carson had called. He'd spoken to the man a few times since the evening he'd seen him at the hospital when Sage was injured. Carson seemed like a good guy, one Justin might even consider a friend when he had time for building friendships. "It's a good time, Carson. What can I do for you?"

"I hate to call you on a weekend, but the pump went out and I've tried everything I know to do to get it running. I was hoping you could come out and take a look at it."

Justin glanced at the clock on the kitchen wall. "Sure. I need to do a few things, but I should be there within an hour."

Carson sounded relieved. "That would be great. The pump in question is past the barn near the pond." Carson gave him directions out to the ranch.

"Okay. Just cut the power to it for now and I'll be there as soon as I can." Justin disconnected the call and hurried to his bedroom where he changed into work clothes. He rushed outside, locked the doors, and jogged toward the shop located about a hundred yards away from the house. Nearly there, he remembered the water he'd left running in the flowerbed and backtracked to turn it off. Once he gathered the supplies he needed from the shop, he loaded his work truck.

To reach the Flying B Ranch, he had to drive through Holiday. After a quick detour to a drive-through window to get a large ice-filled cup of Dr Pepper, he headed on his way.

The ranch was easy to find. As he drove past the house, he noticed Matilda and Ruth sitting on the porch outside. The two old women waved in greeting.

He couldn't help but grin when he thought of

the T-shirt they'd insisted he wear the previous afternoon. If he was the type who embarrassed easily, he might have been horrified when Matilda insisted he show it off to Sage. Unable to read her reaction, he wondered what she really thought of the shirt. Perhaps, more importantly, he wondered what she thought of how the shirt looked outlining the muscles of his arms and chest.

Mindful of his thoughts charging off track again, he dragged them back in line as he pulled up near the pond and saw Carson there with another cowboy and a teenage boy.

"Hey, Justin," Carson said, holding out a hand in greeting. "Thanks so much for coming out on a Saturday. I would have waited until Monday, but I moved the cattle into a different pasture yesterday. This pump keeps the tanks full of water. It was working last night, but wasn't this morning."

Justin looked over, surprised to see Shane Presley there. "Looks like you got a good helper today."

Carson grinned at Shane. "He's decided he'd like to work for me on the weekends in exchange for a calf I gave him for a 4-H project."

"That's cool," Justin said, grinning at the teenager. "How are you doing, Shane?"

"I'm great. Thanks again for your help when Sage was hurt," Shane said, watching his every move as he collected the tools he needed from his rig.

"My pleasure." Justin picked up his tools. "Let's take a look at the pump and see what might be wrong."

Three hours later, Justin had replaced the ancient pump, rewired the electrical panel that was one short away from a fire, and was grateful for the warmth of the spring day because he was soaked in chilly water and coated in mud.

"Man, I can't thank you enough for all the work you did today," Carson said. He was nearly as dirty as Justin. The rancher had sent Shane back to the barn with one of his ranch hands so the boy would stay out of the mud.

"I'm glad I had everything we needed on the service truck to get you up and running. You shouldn't have any problems with this pump for a long, long time."

"I appreciate that," Carson said, helping carry tools back to Justin's pickup. "When you finish the Golden Skies project, maybe you could come out and take a look at some of the other electrical panels around the place. I know for sure some of them need to be updated."

"I'd be happy to do that. If you aren't in a rush, I'll make a note to come out the week after I finish up at the Hokey Pokey Hotel." Justin smirked at Carson. "That is what you call Golden Skies, isn't it?"

Carson chuckled. "Yeah, it is." He glanced at his watch then at Fynlee waving to him from the back porch steps. "I think dinner's ready. Why don't you join us?"

Justin glanced down at his mud-soaked clothes. "I can't track this mess inside your house, Carson."

"We're eating in the backyard, so there's no mess to worry about. If you want, you'd be welcome to borrow some of my clothes."

"I've got a clean shirt in the truck, but I really don't want to impose." Justin did like the thought of eating dinner with people he was coming to consider his friends.

"No imposition at all. Fynlee's grandmother and my aunt Ruth are here today and they've been cooking up a storm. Fynlee made a big potato salad and Sage was going to bring dessert." Carson thumped a gloved hand on Justin's shoulder. "The least we can do is feed you dinner for working so hard all afternoon. I'm sure you had other things you would rather have done today than get coated in mud out here."

"It's fine, Carson." Justin looked over at the rancher. "If you're sure I won't be imposing, I'd be happy to join you all for dinner. Do you have somewhere I can wash up?"

"Come to the barn. There's a bathroom there and we just hose out the mud and crud." Carson led the way to the barn and showed Justin where he could wash up. Justin removed his shirt and stuck his head under the faucet to get out the globs of mud clinging to his hair. When he finished, he took a towel from the stack on a shelf and dried off. He hooked his dirty shirt with one finger and started back to his truck with it.

A startled gasp drew his attention to a woman a few yards away as she approached the barn.

"Hey, Sage. Fancy meeting you here," he said, tossing her a grin before he continued on the way to his pickup.

Chapter Six

Sage carried a lemon Bundt cake to the front door of Fynlee's house and knocked. She wasn't surprised in the least when Matilda opened the door and ushered her inside.

"Sage, darling! We're thrilled you could join us today. It's so lovely outside, we decided to eat dinner out on the picnic table. Won't that be fun?"

"It will be fun." Sage set the cake platter on the counter and smiled at Ruth and Fynlee. "It's so nice of you to invite Shane and me for dinner. Did he behave himself today?"

"Of course," Fynlee said, wiping her hands on a dishtowel then hurrying around the counter to give Sage a hug. "He went with Carson this morning when he was checking the fence in the north pasture. This afternoon, he's been working in the barn. Carson's having problems with one of the pumps and he's out with the electrician to see if they can get it running again."

The mention of an electrician immediately drew Sage's thoughts to Justin James. She wondered if he was the electrician they called. There was another electrician in Holiday, but from what she'd heard, the man's work was as cheap as his prices.

"I can't tell you how grateful I am to you and Carson for allowing Shane to come work here on Saturdays and let him keep Fred Asteer as his 4-H project. He's been like a different boy the last few weeks. I just feel bad that you guys have to take care of the calf during the week."

"It's no problem, Sage," Fynlee said, as she sliced potatoes and eggs into a bowl for a salad. "Carson has three other calves he's bottle-feeding anyway."

"Still, it's so kind of him to let Shane have the calf." Sage picked up a knife and started slicing cucumbers for a green salad.

"Oh, that boy is working hard for Fred Asteer," Ruth said, stirring a dish full of baked beans and returning it to the oven. "He'll earn every cute little hair on Fred's head."

Sage grinned. "Good. I want him to learn the value of hard work and paying his own way."

"He's a good boy, Sage. You're doing an excellent job raising him." Matilda gave her a hug around her shoulders.

The women kept up a lighthearted conversation as they finished meal preparations. Fynlee and Sage draped a tablecloth over a picnic table outside then carried out the dishes.

"Would you mind running out to the barn and letting the guys know dinner is just about ready?" Fynlee asked. She jogged up the porch steps as Sage carried a salad bowl to the table.

"Sure. I'll let them know." Sage set the bowl down next to Ruth's baked beans then walked out the gate. Careful to close it behind her, she didn't want to accidentally let Jack and Gus, Carson's two red heeler dogs, sneak into the yard and snitch the food off the table.

The dogs wagged their hind ends as she stopped to pet them on her way to the barn. She bent down and gave them both gentle rubs and a few scratches that earned her several happy hand licks. Sage stood up and continued to the barn, watching the antics of the dogs. She nearly ran into a shirtless man who suddenly appeared in front of her.

Sunlight shone behind him like a spotlight and Sage sucked in a gulp of air at the sight he made. Muscles unlike anything she'd ever imagined seeing up close and in person drew her eyes to his ripped abs. Her gaze traveled upward to his sculpted chest, bulging biceps, and over the taut muscles of his shoulders and neck. Continuing her perusal, her roving gaze moved to his face. It was then she realized the hunk was none other than Justin James.

He spoke to her, but she was so dazed by his unexpected appearance, she had no idea what he'd said. Her feet and brain refused to function as she remained rooted to the spot, watching him walk down the lane by the barn toward a pickup parked at the pond. Even though he wore dark blue work pants with cargo pockets on the sides, he certainly filled them out well.

She closed her eyes and blinked twice before she regained her senses and continued on her way to the barn. Inside, she found Shane rinsing out the bottle he'd used to feed Fred while Carson washed two other bottles.

"Dinner is ready," Sage said, utterly distracted by the sight of Justin. She thought the vision of him standing in the sunlight without his shirt on might be branded into the recesses of her brain for the rest of forever. Not that she was complaining, but it was rather unsettling.

"Great. I'm starved," Carson said, setting the bottles on a rack to dry.

"Me, too," Shane said as he led the way out of the barn. He glanced over at Carson. "Thanks again for inviting us to stay for dinner."

"We're happy to have you," Carson said, ruffling Shane's hair. He held open the gate to the yard and stopped a moment to pet the dogs before he closed it and hurried inside the house.

"Did you wash up?" Sage asked Shane as she placed her hands on his shoulders.

"Yep. I'm ready to eat. Is Justin going to stay for dinner, too?" Shane asked, glancing behind him as Justin drove his pickup near the house and parked it.

"It appears that way." Sage hoped he put on a shirt. If he ran around shirtless, she wasn't sure she could keep enough brain cells together to eat dinner without spilling it all over.

"Justin!" Shane called, motioning him to come into the yard as he neared the gate in the fence.

"Hi everyone," Justin said as he stepped into the yard and closed the gate. He smiled at Ruth and Matilda, and then Fynlee as he crossed the yard. "Is there anything I can do to help?"

"I think we've got everything," Fynlee said, glancing over her shoulder as Carson hustled down the steps as he tucked the tails of a clean shirt into his jeans. It looked like he'd taken a quick shower in the five minutes he'd been inside the house.

Sage shifted her gaze back over to Justin. He wore a clean button-down shirt with the Holiday Electric logo on the front of it, although he had on the same muddy pants and work boots.

Unexpectedly tongue-tied she had no idea what to say to the man, especially when Matilda and Ruth somehow maneuvered her so she sat directly across from him at the table. They'd placed Shane at the other end of the table close to Carson and one of the cowboys who worked on the ranch.

After Ruth said grace, they all dug into the food. In spite of the nerves churning in her stomach, Sage was hungry and the slow-roasted beef brisket Ruth had made for dinner was excellent. Served with crusty bread, savory baked beans, Fynlee's potato salad, a green salad, and Matilda's specially-seasoned corn, the meal was delicious.

Convinced she couldn't hold another bite, Sage toyed with the few bites of potato salad remaining on her plate while covertly studying Justin. He laughed at something Matilda said then smiled at Ruth as she quietly made a comment.

"What about you, Sage?" he asked, turning the warmth of his rich brown eyes on her.

Caught woolgathering, she felt heat stinging her cheeks in embarrassment. "I'm sorry. I wasn't paying attention. What was the question?"

Justin grinned. "I just asked if you have plans for Easter."

"Nothing exciting. Shane and I will go to church, of course, and then I thought we might go for a drive and take along a picnic." Sage shrugged. "He's declared himself too big for coloring eggs or doing any of the fun things we used to, although I'm not sure he's believed in the Easter Bunny since he came to live with me."

Justin's grin faded and he gave her a curious look before he glanced down the table at Shane. His gaze shifted back to her. "Isn't Shane your son?"

Sage choked on the sip of lemonade she'd just swallowed. Matilda whacked her on the back as she coughed into a napkin. When she ceased coughing and could speak again, she shook her head. "Shane is my brother."

Eyes wide in shock, Justin gaped at her. "Your brother? So you aren't… you don't have… Are you married?"

Had Sage taken another drink, she was sure she would have spewed it all over Justin. It was a good thing she'd merely sat glaring at him in disbelief. What on earth had given him the idea she was married and Shane was her son? How old did he think she was, anyway?

"She isn't married," Matilda said when Sage remained silent. "She doesn't even have a boyfriend right now, do you, darling?" The old woman appeared to size up Justin before she leaned toward him. "Are you interested?"

There were times Matilda needed a muzzle. Sage gave the woman a quelling look, but she was too busy scowling at Ruth who was making shushing motions from across the table with her hands.

Justin's smile returned and he winked at Sage. "I might just be."

Sage's cheeks burned with embarrassment and she ducked her head. Although she wasn't the least bit hungry, she picked up her fork and shoved a bite of beans in her mouth just to keep from having to speak.

"We're too full for dessert. Let's wait a few minutes," Ruth declared as she stood from the table. Purposely, she bumped Justin with her elbow. "Why don't you walk Sage down to the pond and show her what you did today?"

"Sure." Justin stood and gave Sage an inquisitive glance. "If you're game for it."

With every set of eyes at the table staring at her, Sage could hardly refuse. Instead, she stepped away from the table and started across the yard. Justin fell into step beside her. His hand settled on hers as they reached for the latch of the gate at the same time.

"Allow me," he said in a quiet tone as he pushed open the gate.

She hurried through it then continued walking as he closed the gate. He kept his hands in his pockets as he strolled with her to the pond. "Are you upset about something?" he finally asked, breaking the silence that had fallen between them.

Sage shook her head, refusing to admit how greatly his presence disturbed her. Matilda's comments coupled with the fact Justin thought she was old enough to have a teenage son were partly to blame for her unease. Rather than reply, she kept her gaze fastened on the path in front of them.

"Look, Sage, I'm glad to discover the truth about your relationship with Shane and your marital status," he said with a rascally grin. "You have no idea how many times in the last few weeks I've felt horrible for envying the lucky guy I thought was your husband."

Her head swiveled around and she studied him, seeing humor mixed with sincerity on his handsome face. "I had no idea you assumed I was married, or that Shane was my son."

"You seemed awfully young to be his mother, but for all appearances, you make an awesome mom."

Sage blushed. "Thank you. I don't know what I'm doing half the time, but I try. It's important to me to give Shane a solid foundation for his future."

"If you don't mind my asking, how did you end up raising him? Are your parents still alive?" Justin asked as they reached the pond. He pointed to a section of fence and they walked over to it.

Sage leaned her back against a post worn smooth from cattle rubbing on it over the years while Justin rested his forearms on the top pole. Few people knew her background or the whole story of why she was raising her brother, but something about Justin, something she knew she could trust, made her willing to share her past with him.

"Shane is my half-brother. We have the same father, such as he is. My parents married right after they graduated from high school in Portland. They were both into drugs and drinking. Anyway, I came along and they made an attempt at taking care of me, at least for a year or so. Then my mother took off and my dad had no idea how to care for a baby. I ended up in the foster system. My dad would come around once in a great while to see me, but it was usually a brief visit." Sage sighed. Memories washed over her, stirring feelings of anger, hurt, abandonment, and despair.

She glanced at Justin then looked out at the pond. "My mother is serving two consecutive life sentences for murdering a couple in California. She was high and wanted more drug money. From what I heard, she claims she doesn't remember doing it, and she probably doesn't, but it won't change or undo what she's done. When I was eleven, my father came to visit and showed me pictures of a brand-new baby. Shane captured my heart from the start, even if I didn't get to see him in person until he was two when I went to stay with Dad and Shane's mother for a while. I've never been clear if they were married or not. Anyway, that only lasted about six months before Shane's mother died of a drug overdose. Dad tried to take care of us, but he spent more time drunk or high than sober, so it wasn't long until Shane and I were both in the system. I begged them to keep us together, but I got sent one way and Shane another. My social worker would make sure Shane received letters I'd written to him and she even arranged a few visits, but I missed him so much."

"It must have been a hard time for you," Justin said, giving her a compassionate glance.

The last thing she wanted was his sympathy, but the kindness on his face made her continue her story.

"When I was fifteen, I started taking business classes at the community college. By the time I turned seventeen, I had an associate's degree in business administration. I was convinced if I could get a steady job, they'd let me have Shane. The day after I graduated from high school, I started working as an errand girl for a big plumbing company in Portland. A week later, I rented my first apartment and moved out on my own, thanks to a referral by a friend's father who knew the owner of the apartment complex. I begged my social worker to help me get custody of Shane and she went to bat for me, knowing I'd take good care of him. Right after I turned eighteen, Shane came to live with me and a month later, I was named his legal guardian."

Sage bent down and plucked a piece of dry grass, twisting it between her fingers. "I didn't want to raise him in Portland, so I started searching for a job in a smaller town. We moved to Holiday five years ago when I got a job working at Golden Skies. It's been a blessing to both of us to be here, but Shane had a hard time adjusting. He can be withdrawn and bit of a loner, so it's been wonderful to see the changes in him since he's been coming to the ranch the last few weeks. He's been on cloud nine since Carson told him he could keep that calf he's been bottle-feeding."

"Wow, Sage. I can't imagine taking on so much responsibility when you were so young." Justin turned to face her. "You have to be one of the most selfless, inspiring people I've ever met."

Sage shook her head. "No, I'm not. I'm just a girl who cares about her brother."

"You're far, far more than that." Justin reached out and took her hand in his, giving it a squeeze. "You, Sage Presley, are a beautiful person inside and out."

Humility stained her cheeks with a rosy blush. "I'm not doing anything many others haven't already done."

"Most teenagers I know wouldn't sacrifice their youth to be a parent to a half-sibling." Justin tipped her chin up and smiled at her. "Don't sell yourself short. What about your father? Do you ever see him?"

Sage shook her head. "No. Not since we moved here. He moved to San Diego the last time I heard from him. He usually calls on my birthday and Shane's, but that's about it. Until he gets his act together, it's better for all of us if he stays away. Shane doesn't need his influence and Dad knows it, accepts it for what it is."

"I'm sorry, Sage. I can't even begin to imagine how hard it must be to have lived through your past and to have the responsibility of raising your brother."

Desperate to change the subject, Sage turned

and looked at the pond and the cattle in the distance. "It's lovely out here."

"It really is. I can see why Carson wanted to buy the place from Ruth and why Fynlee loves the ranch," Justin said, following the direction of her gaze. "Shane said he's working here on the weekends now. Does that mean you have to make two trips out here every Saturday?"

"Yes, but I don't mind. I wish I could find somewhere to move his calf closer to town, though, so he could see him every day instead of just weekends." Sage continued fiddling with the stalk of grass she held. "He loves taking care of Fred Asteer."

Justin chuckled. "That's a great name for a calf. Did Matilda and Ruth help name it?"

Sage giggled. "How could you tell? The calf has a twin named Ginger but the cow rejected Fred."

"I've got a pasture that's empty if you want to keep Fred there. I wouldn't mind at all and it's close enough Shane could ride his bike over after school."

Sage couldn't believe the offer he'd just made. "Are you serious?"

"Completely. I was just thinking today that I should do something with the pasture, but I had no idea what. I don't have time to care for livestock, but I hate to rent it out to a stranger."

"What would you charge to rent it to us?" Sage asked, hoping Justin wouldn't name a number that was more than she could afford. She managed well enough on her income from Golden Skies, but there was never an abundance of money in her life. She knew, too, that raising Shane would get progressively more expensive as he got involved with sports and other activities in high school. She dreaded the day he started asking for a car to drive. If it hadn't been for Ruth's kindness, Sage would be forced to drive some old clunker that would most likely leave them stranded somewhere.

"How about in exchange for rent, you make me dinner once a month?" Justin asked with a straight face.

Sage scowled at him. "That's not a fair trade in the least and you know it."

"Well, I didn't want to sound greedy and ask for once a week."

She grinned. "Once a week is fair. You tell me what day and I'll make it happen. It still seems like we're getting the better end of this deal, though."

"Then you obviously have no idea how much a single guy appreciates a home-cooked meal." He held out his hand. "Is it a deal?"

She shook his hand, trying to ignore the electrical currents firing up her arm and threatening to short-circuit her senses. "It's a deal. I think we'll have to wait a few more weeks before Fred is big enough to move, but Shane will be thrilled."

"It'll be fun to have the calf there." Justin continued to hold her hand as he studied her face. "I do have one more request, though."

"What's that?" Sage asked, finding herself inexplicably drawn to Justin. Her hands fairly itched to brush across the stubble on his jaw or glide through the tousled locks of his dark brown hair. Although his hair wasn't overly long or shaggy, it was long enough to be a temptation to women. Sage certainly wasn't immune to the desire to bury her fingers in it.

Justin cleared his throat and appeared nervous, but he held her gaze. "Would you do me the honor of going out on a date? I'd love to have you and Shane come over some evening. I'm not a great cook, but I do a decent job with the grill. We could have burgers or steaks."

Sage couldn't believe he'd asked her on a date in one breath and included Shane in the next. The few men she'd dated over the years acted like she had the plague when she made it clear she and Shane were a package deal.

Although she wanted nothing more than to accept Justin's invitation, she knew it wasn't wise to allow any interest to grow between them. Not when her brother needed to be her focus.

However, no one seemed to have informed her wayward tongue of what her head knew. "We'd love to come over. Just let us know what day works for you," she listened to herself say with no small degree of astonishment and dismay.

Justin's grin broadened. "How about Tuesday evening? Would you rather have steaks or burgers?"

"Surprise me," she said, ignoring the inclination to rescind her agreement. Instead, she tossed him a flirty grin before pointing to the pump. "Now, you better show me what you did today or I won't know what to say when Ruth and Matilda interrogate me later."

Justin showed her the new pump and electrical panel. He didn't get technical as he explained what he did, but she could see the project had been a lot of work. And with mud covering the ground it was easy to see how he'd been coated in it from head to toe.

"We probably better get back before Matilda sends Shane out to find us," Sage said, turning toward the path that would lead them to the barn. As they walked together, she glanced at Justin, admiring his rugged profile and broad shoulders. "You know all about the skeletons in my family closet. What about you? Where did you grow up? Do you have siblings?"

Although he didn't touch her as they slowly meandered along the dirt trail, he remained so close to her side, Sage could feel the heat from his body enveloping her in warmth. She cast a quick glimpse to him, admiring the way the setting sun shone around him in a perfect gold and amber glow.

Justin looked at her then shoved his hands in his front pants pockets, as though he needed to keep from reaching out to touch her. Part of Sage wished he would take her hand or drape his arm around her shoulders. The sensible part of her brain loudly objected to the idea.

Justin glanced down at her and shrugged. "I grew up on a pear orchard near Medford, in the southwestern part of Oregon."

"I've seen it on a map, although I've never been there," Sage said. In truth, she'd never been many places. Other than the various cities close to Portland she'd lived in during her years in foster care, and Holiday, she hadn't explored much of the state.

"My parents, sister, and brother-in-law live there." He grinned at her. "And to answer your question, I just have one sister, and she's definitely bossy. Her husband's a great guy and they've been married almost six years. They're expecting their first baby in August."

"That's exciting," Sage said, smiling at Justin. "Do you hope it's a boy or a girl?"

"If I say a boy, you'll probably smack me or something," he teased. "Seriously, I don't care as long as the baby and Janie are healthy."

Sage's smile widened, pleased with his answer. "Are you close to your sister? What was it like growing up on an orchard?"

"Janie's three years older than me and we got along well as kids, for the most part. Did I mention she's super bossy?" Justin asked with a heart-melting grin.

"You did allude to that."

He chuckled then pointed to the sunset, stopping so they could watch the amazing colors filling the sky. "My great-grandparents started the orchard, so it's kind of a family tradition to keep it going. My dad has three sisters and none of them were interested in staying at the orchard, so he and my mom bought the orchard from my grandparents. Janie was always the one who wanted to grow pears, not me. She went to college and studied all sorts of ways to graft and create new varietals. She's got five acres that are just experimental projects. Her husband is as into the orchard thing as she is, so it's good they bought into the partnership and will take over when my folks retire at some point in the distant future."

"That's incredible your family has so much history right there at the orchard." Sage glanced down at the ring on her left ring finger. "The only thing I have from my family is this ring. It belonged to my dad's mother. All I know is that her name was Iris."

Justin took her hand in his and lifted her finger to catch the fading sunbeams. The platinum band sparkled in the light. "It looks old, like something from the Art Deco period."

"You know about Art Deco?" she asked in astonishment.

"I'm not just a big dumb jock," he said, flexing his biceps and making a goofy face that drew out her laugh. "One of the first jobs I had when I was working as an electrician's apprentice was at a home decorated entirely in the Art Deco style. I learned a lot about it the two weeks we were there during a renovation."

Sage wished Justin would flex his impressive biceps again, but she knew he'd done it only in jest. Absently, she pondered if his muscles would feel as hard as they looked. Disconcerted by the direction of her thoughts, she steered the conversation back around to his childhood. "What was it like growing up amid pears?"

"Fruity," Justin said with a straight face then turned to her with a grin. "It was mostly awesome. Things could get intense in the spring if it frosted late in the season because it can damage the buds on the trees. Or if it hailed, which bruised the fruit. Or any number of problems that could impact harvest.

If you take out all those variables, it was a lot of fun and a great way to grow up. My parents are good people and they encouraged Janie and me to pursue whatever interested us. That's why she's the pear whisperer and I'm the electrician."

"So if I go to the grocery store this fall and buy a pear, what are the odds it's from your family's orchard?" Sage asked, intrigued by the idea.

"Slim. My family sells most of their pears to a distributor that places them in stores along the I-5 corridor. Some of them end up in a pear of the month club run by a company based in Medford that sells everything from chocolate covered popcorn to the best chocolate truffles."

"Truffles?" Sage asked with interest. Although she loved chocolate, she tried not to keep much candy in the house. When she purchased it, she considered it a splurge to buy a bag of Hershey's miniature candy bars.

"My sister swears they are the best chocolate candy ever invented. The next time I go home, I'll try to remember to bring you back some."

"Do you go home often?" Sage asked as they neared the barn. Unwilling for their time together to end, she slowed her steps.

"No. I went home for a few days at Christmas, and I'll be there for Easter. One of my cousins is getting married and asked me to be a groomsman, so I'll be gone a few days. I was hoping to have everything finished at Golden Skies before I left, but that's not going to happen."

Sage waved at Matilda as the woman motioned for them to return to the yard. "You're ahead of schedule though, aren't you? I thought I heard the director say something the other day about the project being completed faster than she anticipated."

Justin nodded and opened the gate to the yard. "We're about a week ahead of schedule, but I like to have a cushion in case something unexpected pops up."

"Did you two enjoy your walk?" Ruth asked, placing a hand around Sage's waist and giving her a squeeze.

"You look like you enjoyed it," Matilda said, nudging Justin with her elbow.

Before he could respond, Fynlee carried the cake Sage had made out to the table while Carson followed with a pie in one hand and a carton of vanilla ice cream in the other.

"Ready for dessert?" Fynlee asked as she smiled at Sage.

"I know I am," Justin said, giving Sage a look she found impossible to interpret.

"Do you want lemon cake that Sage made or Ruth's cherry pie?" Fynlee asked Justin.

"A small piece of both?" he said with a boyish grin.

"Give him a big piece of each," Matilda ordered, taking the ice cream from Carson and opening the lid.

Sage watched as Justin tasted the cake and gave her an odd look then took another bite.

"You made this?" he asked, pointing his fork to the moist Bundt cake drizzled with cream cheese frosting.

"I did." Sage tried to gauge if he liked it, and couldn't decide. "Are you a lemon fan?"

"Not usually, but this is amazing. I look forward to our weekly dinner arrangement." He forked another big bite and winked at her causing her stomach to flutter with nerves.

"What arrangement might that be?" Matilda asked, not even trying to hide her nosy interest in their conversation.

Sage knew the woman would pester her until she answered. No sense in putting off the inevitable. "Justin offered to let Shane keep Fred in his pasture if we feed him dinner once a week."

Carson chuckled. "Now that's a good trade." He glanced at Shane. "Would you like to keep Fred in town so you can feed him every day?"

"Boy, would I. That would be awesome." Shane looked at Justin, then turned to Carson. "But I can still come out on Saturdays and work for you, can't I?"

"You bet you can," Carson said, grinning at Shane.

Sage felt a lump lodge in her throat as she watched her brother eat up the attention Carson sent his way. She'd tried so hard over the years to be everything her brother needed, filling the roles of mother and father, but it had become glaringly clear to her Shane still needed a positive male influence in his life. Or maybe more than one, if the way he eagerly hung on Justin's every word was any indication.

She had no idea how she'd find the strength to continue resisting Justin's charms, especially now that she'd committed herself to making dinner for him once a week. On top of that, she'd agreed to dinner at his place Tuesday.

What had she been thinking?

A glance across the table as Justin put his arm around Ruth and gave the older lady a gentle hug made her heart as soft as butter that had been sitting in a summer sun.

Perhaps she'd been thinking she'd finally encountered a guy who might be able to live up to her impossible dreams of finding her very own knight in shining armor.

Chapter Seven

Tuesday afternoon, Justin left Golden Skies at five on the dot and hurried out to his pickup. Since he'd cleaned the house on Saturday and gone to the grocery store yesterday when he left work, he was able to rush straight home and jump into dinner preparations.

He'd told Sage to plan to arrive at six. That gave him fifty minutes to get everything ready.

Crosby practically knocked him down in his haste to get to the garage to eat when Justin opened the door to the deck where he fired up the grill and waited for it to heat. The cat meowed impatiently at the door to the garage, glaring daggers at Justin to hurry up and let him in.

Justin opened the door to the garage and followed Crosby inside, shocked to see the cat's food bowl empty once again. He knew there was a little food left in it when he shooed Crosby out that morning.

Surely a mouse couldn't eat that much food. What kind of critter had invaded the garage? Justin knew he'd have to investigate, but it would wait another day or two.

He fed the cat and watered him, then returned to the kitchen. Chicken breasts he'd left marinating overnight in a special sauce would provide the main course of the meal. He took them out to the grill and carefully placed them. With a quick adjustment to the heat, he hustled inside and turned on the oven. While it heated, he assembled a green salad and returned it to the fridge.

Although he didn't own a tablecloth, he did put placemats on the table before adding plates and silverware. Napkins weren't something he thought to buy, so he ripped three paper towels off the roll near the sink and set them at each place setting.

Salt, pepper and butter went on the table, along with a jar of strawberry jam one of his senior clients had given him last week. He slid a pan of pre-seasoned potatoes into the oven then went outside and flipped over each piece of chicken before returning inside. He'd made a pitcher of lemonade, but wasn't sure if Sage would rather have something else to drink. He had juice, pop, and milk available, too.

Sage had told him that morning that she'd bring dessert, and he gladly agreed to let her. He wasn't sure what to think of her coming over for dinner, if she was interested in him or not. If nothing else, the date would give her and Shane an opportunity to see the pasture and decide if using it was worth feeding him dinner once a week.

Truthfully, he would have let Shane keep his calf there for free, but the possibility of entering an arrangement that guaranteed he'd get to spend time with Sage held too much appeal to ignore. The last thing he wanted was to make more work for her, but he assumed she probably cooked dinner most nights anyway. Besides, after tasting that amazing cake she made the other day, he'd looked forward to sampling more of her culinary skills.

Justin looked around his spacious kitchen and could picture Sage there, laughing at something Shane said as she stood at the sink. Or casting him a look over her shoulder that set his blood on fire.

No matter how much he'd tried to get Sage out of his head, it had been impossible. He was stunned and grateful to discover she wasn't married. Relief had washed over him in a welcome flood when that detail came to light Saturday evening. Justin had felt like a lowlife heel each time he thought of her when he was convinced she belonged to another man. It was wrong and he'd spent plenty of time trying to get her out of his thoughts, sending up prayers for forgiveness for his wayward notions.

The discovery she was single had been a wonderful shock. Sage was unattached and completely available.

Justin didn't plan to let the opportunity to spend time with her slip through his hands. Not when he intended to get to know the beautiful, hardworking, caring, fascinating woman much better.

The fact she'd worked so hard to gain custody of her brother only made him admire her more. Sage was unlike anyone he'd ever met. He couldn't think of any other woman her age who would have given up her teen years to ensure a better future for her brother. As much as he wanted to dislike her father, he had to at least give the guy credit for realizing his children were better off without him in their life.

Considering how much Sage and Shane looked alike, he had to assume they took after their father, otherwise there wouldn't be such a strong resemblance between the two of them.

The way Sage's gorgeous green eyes glimmered with emotion made him want to study them at length. He'd been aware of the surprise and interest in them when she caught him without his shirt after he came out of the barn. Later, when they'd discussed her family, he'd seen the pain and regrets mingling there. He'd also noticed heat and longing in her eyes as they watched the sunset.

The yearning to wrap his arms around her and kiss her had nearly obliterated every ounce of restraint he possessed, but he'd somehow managed to behave himself. He wasn't sure how long he could, though. Every time he saw Sage he just wanted to hold her and love her.

Although they hadn't yet gone on a real date, he knew enough from watching her at Golden Skies to know she was kind and gentle, loyal and generous, dependable and honorable. The very fact she was raising her half-brother spoke volumes about her character.

The only challenge Justin could see was Sage's protectiveness of Shane. The possibility existed that she wouldn't allow a man into her life as long as Shane remained her top priority. He didn't expect her to put Shane anywhere else. Regardless, he hoped she would explore the idea of allowing someone else inside the walls she'd obviously built around her heart.

He buttered rolls he'd picked up at the bakery section of the grocery store and slid them in the oven, checked on the chicken, then realized he still wore his dirty work clothes.

Quickly unbuttoning his shirt, he tossed it in a basket in the laundry room and was heading to his bedroom to change when the doorbell rang.

Without thinking about his half-dressed state, Justin rushed to the door and pulled it open. Sage stood on his front step holding a plastic wrap-covered plate in one hand and a paper bag in the other. Shane shifted off one foot onto the other beside her.

"Hey, you're right on time," he said, smiling at them both and moving back so they could walk inside.

"Your house is awesome," Shane said, stepping into the tiled entry.

Justin grinned at him. "I like it, too, but I can't take credit for it. The man I bought it from renovated most of the house in the past few years. After his wife passed away, he decided to move to Portland to live closer to his daughter."

"From the outside, it looks like something from Mayberry with that cute porch," Sage said, wiping her feet on the doormat and following Shane inside. "Oh, it's a beautiful home, Justin."

"Come on in." He reached out to take the plate and glanced at frosted sugar cookies. "These look great."

"We brought cookies and ice cream," Shane said, gaping at the eighty-five-inch television mounted on the wall above a gas fireplace. "Dude, that's so cool!"

"It's pretty awesome when I want to watch football." Justin grinned at Shane then led the way to the kitchen. He set the cookies on the counter and took the bag of ice cream from Sage, placing it in the freezer section of the refrigerator. He turned back around to see Sage intently observing his every move and realized he was parading around without a shirt on. "Make yourselves at home. I'll be right back."

Justin hastened to his bedroom and pulled on a clean T-shirt and pair of jeans then rushed back into the kitchen. Sage and Shane were both standing at the patio door looking outside at the pasture.

"Do you think that will make a good place for Fred Asteer to hang out?" Justin asked as he stepped behind them.

Sage gazed at him over her shoulder with an undecipherable look on her face. "It's perfect. I see there's even a little shelter in the corner to keep him out of the weather."

"It's gonna be great to be able to see him every day instead of just Saturdays. Carson said he should be big enough to move in another week. Will that be okay, Justin?" Shane asked with a hopeful look on his face. "Are you sure you don't mind me bringing him here?"

"I don't mind at all. In fact, I think it will be fun to look out and see him enjoying the place." Justin set a hand on Shane's shoulder and gave it a squeeze. "With all that rich pasture grass, I'm sure Fred will grow like a weed."

Shane grinned and Sage smiled at him as she turned away from the patio door and looked around his kitchen. "Your house truly is fabulous, Justin. You must enjoy having such a lovely place to come home to at the end of the day."

He nodded, wanting to admit he'd much rather have a lovely woman he loved to come home to, but kept his thoughts to himself. Especially when the woman who continually came to mind was standing on the other side of the island in his kitchen looking entirely too enticing for his own good.

She'd worn her hair twisted back in a bun earlier in the day, but now the golden waves cascaded down her back and around her shoulders. He longed to run his hands through the glossy tresses, to see if her hair felt as soft as he imagined. Regretfully, he ignored the urge and stayed on his side of the kitchen island.

"What can we do to help with dinner?" she asked, breaking into his thoughts.

"If you wouldn't mind checking on the rolls and potatoes in the oven, I'll grab the chicken off the grill." Justin pointed to a drawer next to the stove. "Potholders are in there."

He took a platter he'd set on the counter earlier and went out to retrieve the chicken. The outside was crispy and the thermometer he'd inserted into one piece indicated it was cooked to perfection.

After moving the chicken breasts onto the platter and turning off the grill, he returned inside to find Shane holding Crosby while Sage gently stroked the cat's head. The finicky feline purred so loudly, it sounded like a motor running.

Sage glanced up at him with a smile. "The cat was crying so we opened the door to the garage and let him in. I hope that was okay."

Justin placed the chicken on the counter and covered it with a piece of foil, letting the meat rest a few minutes before they ate. Taken aback by the way the cat cozied up to the two Presley siblings, he couldn't believe Crosby actually let them pick up him. Other than Mr. Currin, he hadn't seen anyone the cat liked well enough to get within touching distance since he'd bought the place. It had taken him two weeks of coaxing to get the cat to even let him pet it. The crotchety old beast looked perfectly content held against Shane's chest while Sage lavished him with attention.

Smugly, Crosby glared at Justin. He could practically see a little cartoon bubble above the cat's head that said, "you've been replaced, minion. Be gone with you."

Justin grinned and took a step closer to Shane, still trying to recover from the sight of the cat being friendly and almost normal in his behavior. "That's Crosby. He came with the house and doesn't usually let anyone get close to him, so you two must be even more special than I realized."

"Really?" Shane asked, rubbing the cat's black

and white mottled fur. Crosby closed his eyes and purred louder.

"Really. He wouldn't even let me pet him for a few weeks after I moved in here." Justin reached out and rubbed his hand over Crosby's head. The cat opened his eyes and stared at him, as though ordering him away. Justin took a step back, aware the cat had no problem reaching out to swat him if he was displeased. "He lives outside, but he eats his meals in the garage, otherwise the other cats in the neighborhood take it all and he goes hungry."

"Oh, that's not nice," Sage said in a singsong voice as she took the cat from Shane and held it up close to her face. "How dare they pick on such a handsome, sweet kitty. You're just a handsome thing, aren't you Crosby. Such a good boy."

Justin almost laughed aloud when the cat batted his eyelashes at Sage, as though he understood and agreed with each word she said.

"You can set him outside and then we'll eat," he said, opening the patio door.

Crosby's eyes narrowed and he glowered at Justin when Sage set him outside. The cat gave him one more indignant glare before stalking over to his water bowl and slapping at the water with his paws before taking a drink.

"Why is he doing that?" Shane asked, pointing to the cat as all three of them stood at the patio door.

"He likes to aerate his water, at least that's what I think he's doing." Justin smirked. "Otherwise, he's just a crazy cat beyond the ability of mere humans to understand or comprehend."

Sage giggled. "He's loveable, Justin, and old, too, isn't he?"

"Yeah. Mr. Currin, he's the man who used to have this place, told me he and his wife got the cat when he was just a kitten and that was sixteen years ago."

Shane turned from watching the cat to wash his hands at the sink. "How old do cats get?"

"Some of them live into their twenties, but I think an average age is between fifteen to eighteen years." Justin didn't want Shane to worry about the cat dying anytime soon. As cranky and persnickety as Crosby was, the cat would probably outlive them all. He opened the refrigerator and took out the pitcher of lemonade. "Would you like lemonade, juice, milk, pop?"

"Milk for both of us," Sage said, overriding Shane's request for pop.

Justin poured three glasses of milk and carried them over to the table in the breakfast nook. Sage had already placed the rolls and potatoes on the table. He turned to set the chicken on the table, but she beat him to it. Justin retrieved the green salad from the refrigerator and then held out a chair for Sage.

He offered a word of thanks for the meal and his guests. The word "amen" had barely passed his lips when Crosby jumped up on the deck railing near the window and began meowing.

"Should we let him back in?" Shane asked, clearly concerned for the cat.

"You can, but I'll warn you this is a game he likes to play. He'll go in the garage for a few minutes and then start yowling to get out. If I put him out, he whines to get back in." Justin motioned toward the patio door. "He can't roam free in the house because he has issues behaving himself."

Sage shot him a curious look.

Justin got up and let the cat in then walked him back to the garage before he returned to the table. "When I moved in, I thought it would be easier to feed him in the kitchen and let him hang out in the house in the evenings. The first evening, he shredded three pillows in the living room, marked his territory on my bed, and hacked up I don't want to know what in the middle of the hallway. Considering the fact he does none of those things in the garage, that's where he's going to stay."

Shane grinned and Sage fought back a smile as they passed food around the table.

When she cut into a piece of chicken and took a bite, her eyes widened and she looked at him in surprise. "This chicken is amazing, Justin. It's so moist and full of flavor."

"Yeah, it's good," Shane said, shoving another bite into his mouth. He took another roll, having devoured the first one, slathered in jam, in just three bites. The boy definitely ate like a hungry teen.

"I'm glad you like it. I can grill meat with the best of them, but don't ask me to cook anything on the stove or in the oven. It will end up dry enough to resole your shoes."

Sage shook her head and forked a bite of potato. "I'm not buying it, Justin. You've got cooking skills and know how to use them."

"I'm not admitting to anything," he said with a

teasing grin. "But I appreciate the compliments on my efforts. This really is about the best I can do."

He turned to Shane and asked him about his day. Most of the dinner conversation revolved around Shane, his classes at school, Fred Asteer, and his work on the ranch.

The cat started to protest the confines of the garage about the time they finished eating. Justin got up from the table and let the cat into the kitchen. Crosby stretched and sauntered across the floor toward the patio door. He was almost there when he made a detour and trotted over to Shane, rubbing against his legs and purring loudly.

Shane sent Justin a questioning glance. Aware of the unspoken question, Justin nodded with permission. The boy picked up the cat and carried him outside. Shane sat on a deck chair while the cat curled against his chest, more contented than Justin had ever seen him.

"I can't believe how Crosby has taken to Shane. It's practically a miracle," he said, smiling at Sage as she helped him clear the table. "He tolerates me out of necessity, but Crosby seems to truly enjoy you and Shane."

"Shane loves animals, always has." She looked over at him as he loaded dishes in the dishwasher. "It was kind of you to keep the cat so he wouldn't have to be uprooted from the only home he's known."

"I felt bad for Crosby. He's not a horrible cat, just one who prefers being grouchy to friendly. At least up until you and Shane arrived to work your magic on him." Justin grinned at her then tipped his head toward the big window overlooking the pasture. "Do you think the pasture will work for Fred?"

"It will be perfect. Shane is so excited to be able to see him every day instead of just on Saturdays." Sage offered him a soft smile. "I still don't think feeding you a meal once a week is a fair exchange for the pasture rent."

"I know. Would every other week work better?" he asked, somehow managing to keep a straight face as he spoke.

Sage giggled and tossed a dishtowel at him.

He loved seeing her happy and carefree, even if it only lasted for a few minutes. She looked so young in that moment, it made his heart ache for her lost childhood and teen years. "If you didn't have other responsibilities," Justin glanced out to the deck where Shane continued to pet the cat before shifting his gaze back to her, "what would you do with your life?"

For the length of several heartbeats, Sage stared at him, appearing dumbfounded. "No one's ever asked that before," she finally said. She leaned against the counter with a thoughtful look on her face, as though she considered a hundred possibilities. Eventually, she released a wistful sigh. "I've always thought it would be interesting to learn about personalities, characteristics, and what makes people tick."

"Like a profiler?" Justin asked, stowing the last of the dishes in the dishwasher and picking up a dishrag to wipe off the counters.

"No, more like a psychologist, so I could help

people be better versions of themselves." She sighed again. "But that takes years of schooling and until Shane is out of college, I need to focus on his future, not mine."

Justin wanted to tell her she deserved to follow her dreams, but he couldn't. Not when she was right to put her brother first since she was his guardian. His admiration for Sage shot up to a whole new level of awe.

Overwhelmed by all she'd sacrificed for her brother, Justin couldn't help but wonder what he would have done in her position. He didn't think he would have been as selfless as she'd been. In fact, he wondered how she managed to stay so upbeat and positive. If he'd had to set aside his dreams and future to care for a sibling, he imagined resentment would definitely play a part in his life.

Not liking the direction of his thoughts, he picked up the platter of cookies and studied the shapes. He grinned as he noticed a light bulb she'd frosted yellow and a lightning bolt that was white. There was a screwdriver, a wrench, and a hammer. "These are interesting cookies."

Sage stared at the plate and slowly lifted her gaze to his. "I came back from lunch yesterday and found a box of cookie cutters on my desk along with a note that I should bake a batch of cookies for you. Although it wasn't signed, I have to assume it came from Matilda and Ruth, mostly Matilda."

Justin chuckled and gave her a commiserating look. "She isn't afraid to express her opinions for sure."

"No, she is not," Sage agreed with a smile.

"But she has a big heart and keeps things at Golden Skies lively."

Justin set the cookies on the table then rinsed the rag in the sink. "You have to give me the dirt on Ruth and Rand. I saw him following her around the other day like a lovesick pup. Does she return his interest or is Rand setting himself up for a broken heart?"

A giggle rolled out of Sage. "Poor Rand is quite smitten with Ruth, but she's still mourning the loss of her husband and not quite ready for a new relationship. With patience and perseverance, I have faith Rand will win her heart and affections."

"I can see the need for a little urgency, though. I mean, they are in their eighties." Justin wiped his hands on a dishtowel then dropped it on the counter. "Would you like to see the rest of the house?"

"I'd love to," Sage said, looking outside to check on her brother. He appeared perfectly content with the cat on his lap. Assured Shane was fine, she followed Justin as he led her through the kitchen to a doorway that opened into a room filled with built in shelves. There was a large oak desk with a computer set up on it and two overstuffed chairs in front of it that looked comfortable.

"This was originally a dining room, but since I don't need a big, formal dining area, it made a great office. There's a small office in the shop, but I do most of my bookwork here." Justin guided her through a doorway on the other side of the room and they were back in the great room. From there he led the way past the entry to a hallway and showed her the two bedrooms and bathroom located on the front end of the house.

He guided her back through the great room and into a short hallway with just one door that opened into the master suite.

"Oh, wow!" she stepped inside and took in the magnificent view of the mountains in the distance through the picture window. Distressed pine furniture looked masculine yet trendy against the pale blue-hued walls. A dark blue upholstered chair in one corner matched the color of the comforter on the bed.

She swung her gaze from the view outside to him. "Did you decorate this yourself?"

"I had a little help from my sister. I sent her pictures from the furniture and paint stores and she shared her wisdom."

Sage smiled and turned to look around the room. An object captured her interest. "That is the coolest thing," she said, walking over to a piece of art hanging on the wall near the door. "What's it made of?"

Justin studied the Art Deco-inspired design on his wall. At first glance, the creative style of the piece almost made it look like a flower, but it was really a series of rectangles joined together in such a way the lines curved and flowed instead of appearing boxy. "It's made out of conduit and joints."

Interest sparked in her eyes as she moved closer to study it. "I've never seen anything like it. Where did you find it?"

Justin took a step closer and traced the curve of one line. "I made it. That wall needed a big statement piece, or so Janie said, so I bent the conduit and added the joints."

Sage gaped at him in surprise before breaking into a beaming smile. "It's official. You are related to Superman because I'm fairly certain there isn't anything you can't do."

Pleased by her comment but slightly embarrassed at the same time, Justin shrugged in humbleness. "You'll find my super powers are extremely limited."

She shook her head and grinned at him. "I'm not buying it." Sage poked her head inside his bathroom. He heard her suck in a gasp. "That's the biggest tub I've ever seen."

"It's kind of like a hot tub. It's got jets and everything," he said, stepping behind her as she studied the massive tub. "If you ever want to try it out, just let me know."

Her head snapped around and she scowled at him, as though he'd just proposed something entirely indecent.

He held up his hands in a show of innocence. "I didn't mean like that." The idea of her joining him in the tub held a great deal of appeal, but he certainly wouldn't voice his thoughts. "I just meant if you ever want to use it, I'd be happy to let you."

"Thanks for the offer," she said, exiting the bathroom as though she couldn't get away from him and the tub fast enough.

Before she could rush from the bedroom, he caught her hand and pulled her around to face him. The evening had gone so well, he certainly didn't want it to end on such an unsteady note.

"Sage, I didn't... I don't want..." Justin didn't know what to say. He wasn't entirely certain what he'd done to send her running, other than tease her about the tub.

That might have been his first mistake. No doubt existed his second was bracketing her sweet face with his hands and gently lifting it up so he could look into her magnetic green eyes that truly did remind him of sage with their pale color.

In spite of the tense way she held herself, longing and heat flickered in the depths of her gaze. His thumbs brushed over her cheeks, not at all surprised by how soft her perfect skin felt beneath his work roughened hands.

One hand found its way around to the back of her head, burrowing into her hair, the other slipped around her waist, subtly pulling her closer.

"Sage..." he whispered, unable to stop from leaning down and brushing his lips over hers with a feather-light touch.

She didn't pull back as he thought she might. Instead, her stiff posture relaxed. Her mouth softened beneath his and she slid her arms around his back, as though she needed to hold onto him for support.

Sparks exploded between them and Justin deepened the kiss. Heat and desire fired his blood until everything around him melted away. All he wanted was to go on kissing Sage, holding her close, for the rest of his life.

"Sage? Justin? Are you in here?" Shane called from the great room.

Startled, they jerked apart. Justin took in Sage's

wide-eyed gaze as her fingers flew to her just-kissed lips. He took a step toward her, but she backed toward the door.

"Coming," Sage said, and hurried from the room.

Justin took a moment to gather his composure before he followed her down the hall. He wasn't sure what had just happened between them. Whatever it was, he wouldn't mind repeating the experience, preferably when Shane wouldn't interrupt them.

The boy was washing his hands when they returned to the kitchen. "Can we have dessert?"

"That's a great idea," Justin said, going to the freezer and taking out the bag with the ice cream. Maybe by the time they finished eating cookies and ice cream, he'd be able to think straight.

"I wasn't sure what flavor you liked, so we got a couple different kinds." Sage removed the plastic wrap from the cookies while Justin took three pint-sized containers of ice cream from the sack.

"What's your favorite flavor?" Justin asked Shane, noticing they had strawberry, fudge ripple, and salted caramel to choose from.

"Fudge ripple," Shane said, taking the carton when Justin held it out to him.

"How about you, Sage? I'm gonna go out on a limb and guess your favorite is salted caramel."

She smiled. "You guessed correctly. Do you like any of these flavors?"

Justin nodded as he took three bowls out of the cupboard and gathered spoons. "I like just about any flavor of ice cream although strawberry is one of my favorites."

"Really? You're not just saying that?" Sage asked as she took the bowls from him and set them on the table while he carried over the other two containers of ice cream.

"Nope. I like strawberry and Neapolitan the best followed by Rocky Road ice cream." Justin waited until Sage took a seat at the table to sit down and lift a lightning bolt cookie from the platter. "These are almost too cute to eat."

"Don't let that stop you," Sage said, removing the lid on the salted caramel ice cream and dipping a spoonful.

Justin bit into the soft cookie with just the right amount of sweet frosting. It was heaven. He took another bite then smiled at her. "This is so good. You can bake for me anytime."

She grinned. "Once a week, remember. Did you decide on what day you'd like to do that?"

"How about Fridays?" Shane asked, joining the conversation. He brushed crumbs from the wrench-shaped cookie he'd eaten from the corner of his mouth with his thumb. "You never date or anything, so Justin could come then. Or maybe we could bring dinner here. It's way nicer than our place."

Sage shot her brother a look that let him know he'd already said more than he should have.

"Whatever day works for you is fine with me, Sage," Justin said, helping himself to another cookie, pretending to ignore the annoyed glances she shot at her brother. "Honestly, other than work, I don't have a lot going on, so anytime is great."

"Fridays are fine. Do you want to come this

week?" she asked, taking another bite of ice cream.

"I can't this Friday. I'm going to my cousin's wedding and to see my folks for Easter. Actually, I'm leaving Thursday morning and won't be home until late Sunday." Justin snitched a bite of her ice cream. She gave him a dubious look, but it didn't stop her from continuing to eat her ice cream, or stealing a bite of strawberry from his bowl.

"Who'll take care of Crosby?" Shane asked, glancing outside at the cat as he lazed on a chair near the grill.

"I was thinking about taking him to the rescue shelter in town. They board on a limited basis."

"But Crosby would hate that," Shane said, turning to Sage. "Can we take care of him? I can feed and water him."

Justin sat back and looked at the boy, and then Sage.

She nodded in agreement. "We'd be happy to watch him while you're gone."

"Are you sure?" Justin asked, unconvinced. "You'd have to let him in to eat in the morning and then again in the evening."

"We're sure," Sage said, smiling first at Shane then at Justin. "We'll take good care of him while you're gone."

Justin got up and opened a kitchen drawer then came back to the table and handed Sage a key. "That opens the side door on the garage. If you want, you're welcome to stay here so you don't have to drive back and forth twice a day. There are two empty guest rooms all ready for you to use."

"No, that wouldn't be right." Sage said,

shaking her head.

"Seriously, you'd be doing me a favor." Justin wondered how he could convince her to stay. He could see she liked the idea. Shane nodded his head in such vigorous enthusiasm it was a wonder the boy didn't give himself whiplash. "I hate to leave things unattended for that many days. If you stayed here, I wouldn't have to worry at all about the place or Crosby."

"Well…" Sage appeared to be teetering on the edge of agreeing.

"Shane could check out the pasture and, if he wanted, he could even work on getting the enclosure ready for Fred."

Sage took one look at the excited, expectant look on her brother's face and sighed. "I guess one weekend wouldn't hurt."

"Yes!" Shane pumped his fist in the air then knuckle-bumped Justin.

After they ate their ice cream and cookies, Justin showed them where he kept the cat food, told them about watering Crosby, and pointed out the switch for the fireplace in case they wanted to use it.

"Feel free to eat whatever you find in the fridge or pantry," Justin said as he walked them to the door. Shane ran outside and over to a small tractor parked by the barn. Justin had used it to plow snow during the winter, but hadn't found a reason to play with it yet as spring arrived.

He glanced down at Sage as they stepped onto the front porch. "Are you sure you're okay with the plan to watch Crosby while I'm gone?"

"It will be my pleasure to keep an eye on Crosby." She looked up at him with an expression he found impossible to read. "Are you sure you want us to stay here while you're gone?"

Justin grinned. It was on the tip of his tongue to say he'd much rather they stay when he was home. It had been fun to have both Shane and Sage at his house, although his particular interest rested in Sage.

In fact, as Shane remained out by the barn, Justin led Sage into the yard and around the trunk of a big maple tree out of the teen's line of sight.

"What are you doing?" she asked on a whisper, giving him a curious look as he peeked around the trunk of the tree to make sure Shane wasn't watching. Assured the boy was entertained with the tractor, Justin wrapped his arms around her again.

"This is supposed to be a date and it just wouldn't be right for you to leave without a goodnight kiss." He grinned at her in the moonlight filtering through the budding branches of the tree.

"I thought perhaps you'd already done more than your share of kissing earlier," she said with a coy smile.

"I refuse to acknowledge or believe you can put limits on the quantity of kisses I want to share with you," he teased, wondering what she'd do if he stole a kiss. Smack him? Hug him? Kiss him back? Set his blood on fire again?

She moved a step nearer, sliding her hands up his arms until they rested on his shoulders. "Then you better make it quick because Shane will only stay distracted so long."

"Yes, ma'am," Justin said before he settled his mouth over hers again. Her lips were cool and tasted sweet from the cookies, with a slight hint of caramel from the ice cream. Blended with the luscious flavor that was uniquely her, Justin didn't know when he'd tasted anything as delicious as her kiss.

He pulled her closer and would have deepened the kiss if he hadn't heard Shane's footsteps crunch on the gravel outside the yard's fence. "I guess that will have to last me for a while."

"I suppose it will," she said. Her eyes were hooded and held a dreamy look as she placed a hand on his cheek and gently kissed his lips one more time. "Thank you for everything, Justin. This was one of the nicest evenings I've had in a long time."

"My pleasure. I'm glad you and Shane could come over." Justin took her hand and led her around the tree and over to the gate in the fence that he always left open. Someday, when he had little ones underfoot, he'd be glad for the gate that kept them safely in the yard. A picture of a little boy with Sage's green eyes and his dark hair slammed into his thoughts and left him reeling.

He barely knew the woman. What in blazes was he doing planning his whole future with her? It was crazy, wasn't it?

"Thanks for dinner, Justin, and letting us play with Crosby. It was fun," Shane said as he grinned at him.

"I had fun, too, Shane," he said, setting a hand on the boy's shoulder. "I'm glad you and Sage could join me. And I really appreciate you taking care of Crosby this weekend." He glanced over at Sage as she stepped beside him. "You have the key I gave you?"

"Yes. I already added it to my key ring so I wouldn't lose it," she said, holding up her key ring on one finger.

"Great." He extended his hand to Sage. "Would you let me see your cell phone?"

"Okay," she said. In spite of sounding a little wary, she pulled her phone out of her purse and handed it to him.

Justin quickly added his information to her list of contacts. "If you need to reach me while I'm gone, you've got my number."

"Oh, thank you. I didn't think of that," Sage said, taking the phone and scanning his information. "I'll send you a text so you have mine." She tapped a quick message and hit send.

Justin's phone buzzed in his pocket. He took it out and read the message with a grin. "You, too, Sage."

"What did you say?" Shane asked, trying to see the screen of Justin's phone.

Sage gave him a nudge toward the car. "That's between the grownups." She turned and winked at Justin.

He hurried to open her car door and managed to kiss her cheek while Shane was buckling his seatbelt. "Have a great evening, Beautiful." His voice sounded husky to his own ears as he spoke.

Her hand trailed over his jaw before she slid inside the car and drove away with Justin's heart.

Chapter Eight

Sage unlocked the door to Justin's garage and stepped inside with Shane right behind her. Before they closed the door, Crosby darted inside. His motor began running the moment he brushed against Shane's legs.

The boy laughed and dropped the duffle bag he carried, picking up the cat as it loudly purred. "Hey, Crosby. Did you miss me?"

The cat meowed and snuggled against him.

Sage rolled her eyes, wondering how she'd tell Shane no when he started asking for his own cat. Maybe he could temporarily adopt Crosby since he'd soon be coming over to see Fred every day anyway. Carson had agreed to their plan and suggested moving the calf the following week.

"I'll carry our stuff inside if you want to feed the cat," Sage said to Shane as they moved toward the door that opened into the house.

"Do you suppose he licked his bowl clean this morning?" Shane asked as he stared at the food bowl that held not a single crumb of food.

"Maybe he was really hungry," Sage said, noticing an array of mouse traps set around the garage that hadn't been there on Tuesday. She didn't like spiders or creepy crawlies of any type. Reptiles made her squeamish. But rodents... rodents completely freaked her out.

With eyes wide, she cautiously opened the door into the laundry room and flicked on the light. She carried her bag and Shane's into the kitchen and set them on the floor then looked all around the space to make sure no traps were present, or worse — evidence a mouse had paid a house call.

Nothing appeared amiss, but she still wasn't convinced. She took her phone from her purse and sent Justin a text.

Mouse problem in the garage?

In less than a minute her phone rang. She didn't even bother to look at the caller ID. As soon as she got home from Justin's place Tuesday evening, she'd set the theme song from *The Greatest American Hero* as a special ringtone for him.

"Hey, Justin. You didn't need to call me back," she said, sitting down at the table in the breakfast nook. "I'm sure you are knee deep in wedding plans."

"Almost that deep, but I've got a few minutes to spare," he said. The sound of his deep voice made her smile and warmed her from the inside out. "I forgot to tell you I set mouse traps all over the garage this morning before I left. I don't know for a fact there is a mouse in the garage, but Crosby's food dish is magically emptying itself. I don't think a mouse would do that, but I'm not sure how anything bigger could sneak in. I'll deal with it when I get home, so please don't worry about it."

"Do we need to worry about Crosby getting into the traps?" Sage asked.

Justin's chuckle carried over the connection and she could clearly picture the way his eyes would twinkle with humor. "That crazy cat is terrified of mice and the traps. He sniffed a trap this morning then hightailed it as far away as he could get from it."

"So much for a big, brave cat to protect us from unwanted rodents," Sage said with a giggle.

"Are you two settled in? Is there anything you need?" Justin asked.

"We just got here. Shane is with Crosby in the garage. Crosby started purring as soon as we walked in the door." She leaned back in the chair, wishing Justin was there with them. "I'm going to whip up some dinner, and then Shane has a backpack full of homework that will require our attention the rest of the evening."

"Sounds like fun," he teased. She heard voices in the background and Justin shouted something then he whispered. "I sure miss you, Beautiful. Although I hate to cut this short, we're on our way to dinner with my aunt, uncle, and cousins. Call me if you need anything."

"I will, Justin, and thank you." Sage disconnected the call, still smiling. Although she only saw Justin briefly at lunch yesterday while they ate sandwiches together, he'd called her beautiful and kissed her cheek before he went back to work. Each time he called her that, it felt like her toes might curl inside her shoes while her heart dripped into a syrupy puddle at her feet. Sage didn't think she was beautiful, but Justin made her feel that way.

In fact, he made her feel smart and capable and a better version of herself. However, she needed to stop daydreaming about him and get her head back on straight where he was concerned. No man in his right mind would willingly saddle himself with a teenager plagued by abandonment issues and a woman who wasn't much better.

Regardless of how much she liked Justin, of how easy it would be to fall for him, she had to stay focused on Shane.

But, for the next few days, she intended to enjoy her mini-vacation at Justin's house. The little house she and Shane rented was clean and safe, but it was a far cry from the wonderful home where Justin lived. Shane had mentioned that morning how staying there would be like a vacation for them both. With the big screen TV, leather couches, huge yard, and expansive kitchen, she had to agree with her brother. Sage thought she might even take up Justin's offer for her to use the tub in his room. The idea of relaxing with all those jets while she read a book was far too appealing to resist.

"What's for dinner?" Shane asked as he

bounded into the kitchen, still holding Crosby.

"Chicken. Justin said he had plenty left over from the other night." She washed her hands and opened the refrigerator door. "Did you let Crosby eat?"

"Yeah, I fed him. He ate some of the food, but seemed more interested in being held and petted."

"Why don't you take him outside? It's warm right now. The two of you could sit in the sunshine until dinner is ready."

"Okay," Shane said, taking the cat outside with him to the deck.

After they ate, did the dishes, and escorted Crosby back to the garage, Sage and Shane sat at the table. Sage balanced her checkbook while Shane did his math problems. Although she made him do his homework on his own, she always sat with him while he worked. In case he needed help she was available, but her presence also kept him on task.

He finished his assignments an hour later. The two of them indulged in bowls of ice cream before they let Crosby out of the garage. His food bowl was once again completely clean.

"Let's try an experiment," Sage said, scooping a cup full of flour from the canister she found in the pantry. She took the flour out to the garage and sprinkled it on the floor all around the cat's food bowl then tossed a handful of food into the bowl.

"What's that for?" Shane asked, giving her a curious look.

"To see if we can figure out what's stealing Crosby's food." Sage stepped back and surveyed her work. With the flour dusting the floor all around the bowl, if something was carrying food away, prints would definitely show up.

"Cool! This is like an animal version of CSI." Shane grinned and followed her back into the kitchen.

The next morning, they both hurried into the garage. Tracks in the flour circled the empty food bowl and headed toward the door of a room Justin had said housed the furnace. Shane glanced at Sage then slowly opened the door. Nothing furry scurried over their feet, so Sage felt along the wall and flicked on the overhead light. She didn't see any evidence of a rodent in the room. No weird smells, like a mouse had invaded the space, assaulted her nose.

The room was small and warm. The furnace took up all the space on one side of the door. A set of shelves holding a variety of boxes was on the other while a set of luggage stood in front of them. All appeared normal, so she shut the door and went back to study the tracks.

"Aren't they kind of big for a mouse?" Shane asked, hunkering down to get a better view.

"That's what I think, too." Sage hurried back inside the house and grabbed her phone. She snapped a few photos of the tracks before sweeping up the flour.

"Let's feed Crosby and get ready," she said, giving Shane a nudge back inside the house.

She sent Justin a text with photos of the tracks. He sent a message back asking if they caught anything and she told him they hadn't.

That evening when they returned to the house,

Shane rushed into the garage and checked all the traps, finding them untouched. The food bowl was once again completely empty, though.

"Maybe it's a raccoon, for as much food as it eats," Shane said.

Sage glared at him. The thought of facing a mouse made her want to jump on a chair and scream, but a raccoon might send her racing out the door.

"You feed the cat while I make dinner," she said, carrying in a few bags of groceries. As a thank you to Justin for letting them stay at his house, even if they were taking care of the cat, she would leave a few easy to reheat meals in the freezer for him.

Tonight she was making a chicken casserole and planned to double the recipe, freezing half of it. Tomorrow, she planned to let beef stew simmer all day in a slow cooker she'd brought from home.

Sunday was Easter. Fynlee and Carson had invited them to come out to the ranch for lunch after church services. Justin would be home that evening.

Sage hurried to make the casseroles and pop them in the oven. While they baked, she made a green salad and set the table for the two of them.

Shane went outside and got Crosby. He carried the cat into the garage and returned to the kitchen. After washing his hands, he poured himself a tall glass of milk and drained it before pouring a second glass. Instead of wandering off to watch TV, he dug his homework out of his backpack.

Ever since Carson said his mom made her boys do their homework on Fridays instead of waiting until Sunday evening, Shane had faithfully completed his as soon as he got home from school on Friday afternoons. Sage was thrilled over her brother's new perspective on getting his homework out of the way instead of procrastinating. Sunday nights used to be a battle of wills, mostly hers being tested as she fussed at Shane to finish his homework.

Peace had reined Sunday evenings the last few weeks and she loved that they now spent that time just hanging out together.

"Do you have much homework this weekend?" she asked as she set the salad bowl on the table.

"No. Just math and I have to write a three-hundred-word essay about a topic of my choice."

Sage lifted an eyebrow. "What are you going to write about?"

Shane shrugged, refusing to meet her gaze. "It's probably dumb."

"What is? What do you want to write about?" She placed her hand on his shoulder and gave it an encouraging squeeze.

"Heroes. I want to write about real-life heroes." He glanced up at her with hope in his eyes. "Is that stupid?"

"Not at all," she said, giving him a hug around his shoulders, wondering when they'd started filling out. Shane was one of the biggest kids in his class. She could just picture the broad-shouldered man he'd someday be if he filled out his lanky form. "You'll do great with it. Have you started it yet?"

"Yeah, I had some time at school to work on it today. I'm gonna finish my math first, though." Shane turned his attention back to his math homework while Sage finished getting dinner ready.

After they'd eaten, she did the dishes, while he completed his math assignment. "Do you want help with your essay?" she asked as she dried her hands and hung the dishtowel on a hook by the sink.

"No, I'll do it by myself. Why don't you go read a book or something," Shane said over his shoulder, dismissing her.

"Maybe I will," she said, wandering into Justin's office where books and an eclectic collection of items lined the built-in shelves. She found a James Patterson novel she hadn't read and took it to the great room where she curled up on a corner of the couch and lost herself in the story.

An hour later, Shane plopped down beside her and handed her the laptop he used for his homework.

Sage set aside the book and turned her attention to his essay. Tears stung her eyes as she read Shane's thoughts on her being a hero.

"Oh, kiddo, this is..." Sage couldn't speak when a lump of emotion lodged firmly in her throat.

Shane gave her a hug and pulled back with a grin. "Does that mean you like it?"

"I love it," she said, hugging him again. "You make it sound like I'm practically Wonder Woman."

"Well, if you got a pair of red boots and the thing she wears," Shane motioned toward his chest, "you could be."

Sage laughed and wiped her tears away with the pads of her hands. "I think I'd need to grow about five inches and spend at least three years fully dedicated to working out hours every day, but I appreciate you saying so. Truly, Shane, this essay means so much to me. I know I mess up, a lot, and I'm not an ideal parent, but I love you and would do anything I can to help you grow up to be a good person."

"I love you, too, Sage. You didn't have to take me in when you did and you don't have to sacrifice so much for me, but you do. I know I can be a jerk sometimes, but I'm glad we're together. I couldn't ask for a better mom than the one I already have."

Tears rolled down her cheeks as she wrapped him in another hug and kissed his cheek.

He squirmed against her and pulled away then teasingly wiped his cheek. "Yuck! Save that slobbery stuff for Justin."

Sage's eyes widened in shock that Shane had noticed her interest in the hunky electrician.

"What? Don't give me that innocent look," Shane said, grinning at her. "I know you like him."

"It's okay, Shane. I'm not planning on getting involved with him. You don't…"

Her brother interrupted her by placing a hand over her mouth. "Justin is a great guy, Sage. I'm old enough to know how things work. I don't mind if you like him and want to date him."

Before she could reply, Shane took the laptop and returned to the kitchen. Sage followed him and made a cup of tea.

"Think I'll get an A from this?" he asked, glancing at her as he tucked his papers into his backpack.

"If you don't, I'll pay your teacher a visit and

demand to know why."

Shane groaned. "Don't do that! That last time you got mad and talked to the teacher my life was horrible until school released for the summer."

"It was two days before summer break started in your fourth-grade year. And that teacher was a moron." Sage took a sip of her tea. "What time do you need to be at the Flying B tomorrow?"

"I told Carson I'd be there at eight-thirty. Is that okay?" Shane glanced up at her then hit submit to turn in his homework. He closed his laptop then helped himself to a cookie from a resealable bag Sage held out to him.

"Sure, I can have you there on time." Sage counted any day she could stay in bed past six sleeping in. She wouldn't have to get up until half past seven to get dressed and take Shane out to the ranch.

The two of them spent an hour watching TV then Sage told Shane he better get ready for bed. He escorted Crosby outside then went back to the garage. He remained in there so long Sage went to check on him.

He'd positioned mouse traps all around the food bowl and placed a few over by the furnace room door, too.

"Think we'll catch something?" she asked, backing toward the door.

"I hope so. It would be great if Justin came home and we caught whatever it was," Shane said, returning with her to the kitchen. "Have a good night, sis."

"You, too, kiddo. And for the record, the essay

you wrote is my most favorite thing I've ever read."

"Thanks, Sage." Shane gave her one of his bear hugs that threatened to crack ribs and deprive her lungs of air, but she loved it just the same.

The following morning, Sage awakened to Shane's triumphant shouting. She scrambled out of bed and raced to the garage. Still in his pajamas, her brother stood over a trap that held the biggest mouse Sage had ever seen. She might have mistaken it for a rat, but it was definitely a mouse.

A shudder coursed over her. Shane shot her a gleeful look. "We caught it! Justin will be surprised. This is so cool!" Shane raced past her back toward the kitchen. "I'm gonna take a photo."

"Of course you are," Sage said, carefully peering at the dead mouse without getting too close to it. She knew someone needed to take it out and empty the trap, but the thought of touching it gave her a bad case of the heebie-jeebies.

"Can I send the photo to Justin?" Shane asked after he snapped several shots.

"Yes, but first we need to eat breakfast and get ready to go." Sage didn't bother to take a shower. She pulled on a pair of jeans and an old T-shirt, wadding her hair into a messy bun, and made French toast with bacon for breakfast. While it cooked, she put the ingredients for beef stew in the slow cooker and turned it on.

She programmed Justin's number on Shane's phone and made him promise not to abuse the privilege of having it.

"I won't, but I know Justin will want to see the dead mouse." Shane excitedly sent the photo. He started to pick up the trap, but Sage pushed him back.

"Don't touch that thing! It could be diseased!" She grabbed a broom and swept the trap, mouse and all, into a garbage bag, then deposited it in the big trash bin outside before she took Shane to the ranch.

After dropping him off, she returned to Justin's house and moved the traps away from the food bowl then let Crosby in to have his breakfast. While he ate, she cautiously opened the door to the furnace room and flicked on the light.

Nothing appeared out of place and the room didn't smell like a mouse had invaded it, but just as she was about to turn off the light, she noticed a piece of cat food by one of the suitcases.

She moved the suitcase and her eyes widened as she took in a pile of cat food the mouse had packed beneath the shelves and hidden behind the suitcases.

Sage rolled the suitcases out of the room and surveyed the spill of cat food coming from beneath the shelves. Uncertain what to do with it, she stepped out of the room to consider her options. Loud crunching drew her back into the room. Crosby munched on the cat food the mouse had slobbered all over like it was the last meal he'd ever receive.

"Crosby! Eww! Get out right now. Don't eat that!" she said, shooing the cat out of the room.

He glowered at her and marched over to the door. The feline released a yowl that made his displeasure with her quite evident.

Sage let him out, took her phone from her

pocket, and returned to the furnace room. After snapping a photo, she sent it to Justin along with a message.

Your doomsday mouse was preparing for the apocalypse!

A full minute hadn't passed before her phone rang with Justin's ringtone. "Hey, aren't you busy with wedding stuff this morning?" she asked.

He laughed. "I'm being poked and pinned into a tux at this very moment, but I had to call. So the mouse that Shane was excited about catching was storing food in the furnace room. I can't believe it was hoarding food in there and I didn't even notice. Then again, I don't go in there very often. Is that cat food packed under the shelves?"

"It is. I was just going to see if I could sweep it out," Sage said, giving the mess in the furnace room another glance. She would die if the mouse had a friend still hiding in there. Or babies. At that thought, she shut the door and ran into the house.

"Don't bother with it, Sage. I'm just so glad you caught the mouse. I'll pull out a shop vacuum when I get home and suck it all up. It won't take long to clean up the mess."

Sage could do that and save Justin the work. "I owe you a mousetrap, though. I tossed the whole thing in the trash."

Justin chuckled. "That's okay, Beautiful. I've got plenty."

"So I noticed." She wished she could spend an hour on the phone with him, just listening to his deep voice, but she knew he had a busy day ahead of him. "I better let you go. Have a wonderful time at the wedding."

"I will. I just wish you were here with me. My cousin's fiancée has some really awful bridesmaids. I'm gonna get stuck with one of them for the afternoon."

"Oh, you'll enjoy every minute of it," Sage said, feeling better about knowing Justin wished she was there and one of the women at the wedding had not yet turned his head. Not that she should care, but she did.

"I really do wish you could have come with me. Maybe next time you and Shane will ride along."

Sage couldn't believe he'd included Shane in the invitation, like it was the most natural thing in the world. It was to her, but she didn't think that extended to anyone else. "It might be fun."

"I promise I'd make it that way. Ouch!" he said and mumbled something she couldn't hear. "I gotta go, Sage. I'll call you after the wedding."

"Have a great time!"

She left the phone on the kitchen counter and went back out to the garage. A shop vacuum beneath a work bench along the far wall looked like it would easily handle the job of sucking up all the cat food. She dragged it across the floor and around Justin's work pickup that was parked in the garage. After plugging it in, it roared to life. It didn't take very long to suck up the cat food she could reach.

To get back in the corners against the wall, she had to get down on the floor and shove the nozzle under the shelves with her arm half buried beneath it. She cringed the entire time, but within fifteen minutes, the job was completed. Then she noticed a few mouse pills on the bottom shelf.

"Oh, yuck!" she said, wrinkling her nose in disgust.

She considered closing the door and leaving the mess for Justin, but she couldn't do that. Instead, she hurried to the grocery store and bought a pair of elbow length rubber gloves, disinfectant wipes, and a bottle of bleach spray. Sage stopped at the hardware store and purchased an inexpensive respirator mask then went back to Justin's.

With the mask covering her nose and the gloves pulled up to her elbows, she carried all the boxes on the shelves into the garage and wiped each one down with disinfectant wipes. When the shelves were empty, she concluded the mouse had only used one bottom corner to do his business. After saturating the spot with bleach, she cleaned it up, then wiped all the shelves. She realized the shelves could be moved, so she slid them away from the wall and discovered more cat food the mouse had packed between the lip of the bottom shelf and the wall. She sucked it up then looked around to make sure she hadn't missed any cat food.

Sage took the top off the vacuum and carried the heavy base outside where she dumped it in the big garbage container. She thought there had to be at least ten pounds of cat food.

The thought that the mouse really was planning for the end of the world made her grin as she returned to the garage, stowed the vacuum where she'd found it, and then sprayed the entire floor of the furnace room with bleach. As soon as it dried, she returned the boxes to the shelves. She was almost finished when she noticed one of the boxes had a "photographs" label on the side. Since it wasn't taped shut, she opened the flaps and looked down at a framed image of Justin as a boy.

He was adorable with a mop of dark hair going every which way and his eyes sparkling with mischief. As she stared at the photo, she could envision a little boy looking just like that, except with her green eyes.

Unsettled by her thoughts and how clear the picture of that boy was in her head, she closed the box, hauled the garbage she'd made cleaning the room outside, then went to take a shower and wash her hair. It took two complete showers before she felt clean after dealing with the fallout of the doomsday mouse.

Although she'd planned to spend the afternoon doing something frivolous, like soaking in Justin's big tub with a book and pile of Easter candy she'd snitch out of the basket she'd prepared for Shane, she instead went to the kitchen and made a bunch of food. She took a cake out of the oven just in time to hurry out to the ranch to pick up Shane.

They returned to Justin's place, ate dinner, laughed over the mouse, and watched an Easter movie before going to bed. Sage waited until she was sure Shane was asleep to leave his Easter basket on the counter in the kitchen.

The next morning, he once again awakened her with happy shouts, but this time over the goodies in his basket. Before she could roll out of bed, he raced into her room and jumped on the mattress beside her.

"You are awesome!" he said, giving her a hug with one hand since the other still held his Easter basket.

"What did the Easter bunny bring you?" she asked, feigning innocence of the contents as she scooted back against the headboard.

He gave her a dubious look, but pulled out a set of earbuds, a pair of sunglasses he'd been begging to get, a wallet with a five-dollar bill tucked inside, and an assortment of his favorite candy.

"Looks like you got quite a haul," Sage said, snitching a pink jellybean from the basket.

He nudged her with his elbow. "You better come see what he brought you."

Sage gave him a baffled look, but got out of bed and followed him to the kitchen where an envelope with her name rested on the counter. She opened it and grinned at a silly drawing of an Easter bunny with a chicken and read the funny message. But it was Shane's brief but heartfelt words about how much he appreciated her that threatened to bring tears to her eyes. He'd even included a gift card to the coffee shop.

"Thank you, Shane. This is so sweet."

"You're welcome."

When her cell phone rang with Justin's ringtone, Shane gave her a knowing look and disappeared down the hall.

"Happy Easter!" she said when she answered the phone.

"Happy Easter to you, too," Justin said. "Are you and Shane getting ready for church?"

"We aren't yet but will be soon," she said, glancing at the clock on the wall. They had plenty of time to get out the door. "Are you still at your folks' place?"

"Yep. We just got back from a sunrise Easter service. We're eating brunch then I'm taking off."

It sounded like someone said something in the background. Sage could hear the sound of a door squeaking and slapping shut then all was quiet. "Sorry about that," he said. "My brother-in-law thinks he's a real comedian. I don't want to burst his bubble and tell him the truth."

Sage grinned, envisioning Janie's husband giving Justin a hard time. "How was the service?"

"Really nice and the weather is cooperating today, so that's a good thing," Justin said, then cleared his throat. "The reason I'm calling is because the Easter bunny may have left a little something for you and Shane at my house. If you look in the closet by the front door, you'll see two gift bags on the floor."

"You didn't need to do that, Justin. I feel like you've already done so much for us," she said as she walked through the great room to the entry closet. She opened the door and spied a small bright pink gift bag with sparkly pink tissue paper and a large blue bag with plain white tissue paper. Grabbing both bags, she carried them over to the couch where Shane sat flipping through channels on the TV and handed the blue bag to him.

"Shane's opening his present right now," she

said, watching as her brother ripped out the tissue and pulled a cobalt blue halter from the bag along with a book about raising farm animals.

Shane grabbed the phone from her hand and spoke to Justin, thanking him for the gifts. She could tell from the tone of her brother's voice he loved the halter for Fred and the book that would help him learn more about raising a calf.

While he talked to Justin, she removed the tissue from her gift bag and took out a bracelet made of copper wire. The loops and curls formed a distinctive Art Deco pattern. She slipped it on her wrist and it fit perfectly. She took the phone back from her brother.

"Did you make this?" she asked, holding out her wrist and admiring the bracelet.

"I did. I know you like Art Deco and I was playing with some wire the other day. It just seemed like something you might enjoy," Justin said.

"It's incredible and I love it. Thank you so, so much!" She wished he was there to thank in person. Or hug. Definitely kiss.

"You're welcome, Beautiful. You and Shane have a great Easter and don't worry about leaving. You know you're welcome to stay as long as you like."

"Oh, we'll be gone by the time you get home, but Crosby will be fed." She looked at the bracelet again. "Thank you for making our weekend and especially our Easter so special."

"It's my pleasure, Sage. I'll give you a call when I get home."

"Okay. Talk to you later and drive safely."

She disconnected the call and studied the work of art encircling her wrist. Shane bumped against her with his arm and grinned. "I could be wrong, but I think Justin kind of likes you."

The problem wasn't in wondering if Justin liked her. Sage's concern rested solely in what she should do about it.

Chapter Nine

Justin stepped out on his deck with a cup of coffee. He took a long sip and watched the sun rise over the pasture where one cute little red and white calf ran through the dew-coated grass.

Fred Asteer, Shane's 4-H project, had taken up residence in the pasture a month ago. Justin enjoyed seeing the calf there. In spite of his promise to Sage to not help Shane with his project, Justin found himself out in the pasture, petting the calf and letting it suck on his fingers. There was nothing quite like the milky grass smell of little Fred's breath. Most people would probably find it gross, but Justin liked the scent. It reminded him of happy days on his parents' farm when he'd had his own 4-H projects.

He'd wondered about the calf being lonely, but Fred seemed perfectly content there. Not only that, but Crosby had decided the calf was his own personal pet and could be found curled up with Fred in the enclosure on the far end of the pasture. Justin had improved the two-sided building by adding a third wall and placing a new tin roof over it. No matter how much it rained or the wind blew, Fred had a dry, warm bed of straw in his shelter.

Justin grinned as Crosby tip-toed his way across the damp grass. For a cat who liked to stand with two feet in his water dish, he sure hated to get his toes wet by any other means.

"Get to stepping, Crosby, if you want your breakfast before I leave for work," he called to the cat.

As though he understood each word, the cat meowed and ran the rest of the way to the house then bounded up the steps of the deck.

"Did you and Fred have a good night?" Justin asked as he opened the door and the cat marched inside, heading straight for the garage.

Justin followed him and measured a scoop full of food into the cat's bowl. He glanced around, glad to see the few mouse traps he'd left in strategic spots remained empty.

When he returned home Easter weekend, he'd been dreading cleaning up the mess the mouse created in his furnace room. He opened the door to the faint smell of bleach and a note from Sage taped to a shelf where he couldn't miss it, letting him know she'd removed all the cat food, wiped down the boxes and shelves, and even sprayed the cement floor with bleach. The room was probably more sanitary than it had ever been. Justin still couldn't believe he'd missed seeing the mountain of cat food when he'd grabbed a duffle bag to pack for the weekend.

He'd gone inside the house to find Sage had left one of her lemon Bundt cakes in the refrigerator as well as a dozen individually-packaged home-cooked meals in his freezer.

His offers to pay her for her work and the food were met with a cool glare when he tracked her down at Golden Skies the following morning.

"Staying at your house was a treat for us, so we'll call it a fair trade," she'd said. Justin didn't see anything fair about it all. And he felt guilty each Friday when he showed up on her doorstep for dinner. But not guilty enough he'd stay away.

In fact, she'd invited him to the pizza place tonight for dinner to celebrate Shane's last day of school. Justin well remembered that anxious, excited feeling of anticipation he experienced each year when school released at the end of May. He'd always had a long list of fun things he planned to do over the summer, even if he rarely accomplished more than one or two of them. Summers were busy, yet lazy, wonderful days, when he was a boy growing up surrounded by acres and acres of ripening pears.

His family generally kept between two to three dozen head of cattle, as well as chickens and sometimes pigs. They'd always had a few horses that he and Janie could ride, too. Life had been idyllic in many ways.

Did Sage have any good memories from her childhood? The little she'd shared with him, and the abundance she'd left unspoken, made him question if she'd had any lighthearted moments just to be a child. From the way she wore responsibility like a comfortable old shoe, he assumed she'd probably never had many experiences to just enjoy a carefree existence.

Regardless of her past, Justin was more interested in her future. Specifically, her future with him.

Shane had dropped several less-than-subtle hints that he was more than ready to welcome Justin into the Presley family. It meant a lot to him that Shane liked him and respected him. He wouldn't dream of pursuing a relationship with Sage if Shane hated him. It would have been too hard on her.

Fortunately, Shane got along with him incredibly well. Justin tried to bridge the gap between friend, brother, and father-figure without making Shane feel like he was trying to step into a position the boy didn't want filled. So far, they'd found a good balance.

But for every step Justin tried to move forward with Sage, she seemed to take one back or to the side. It seemed as though she didn't want to get too far away from him, yet she avoided moving forward.

In the grand scheme of things, they'd only been dating about six weeks, but it was more than enough time for Justin to know Sage was *the one.* He wanted to spend his life with her, making her smile, making her feel cherished, surrounding her with his love. He could picture them growing old and gray together right there on his little acreage. Shane would keep them on their toes until he left for college and by then Justin hoped they'd have a little one or two running around.

When he bought Holiday Electric in the autumn and moved to town, he was in no hurry to settle down. He certainly hadn't been looking for a woman who was raising a child, even if that child was her brother.

But he loved Shane and Sage. The thought of both of them coming to live with him made him wish Sage would realize and accept she didn't have to handle all the responsibilities of parenting Shane on her own. Justin knew the Presley siblings were a package deal and it was one he was more than willing to take.

However, the few times he'd tried to broach the topic with Sage, she cut him off or abruptly changed the subject.

Obviously, she needed more time to come around to the idea of him wanting to marry her and help her raise Shane. If it took another month or year, he wasn't going anywhere.

Although, as much as he longed to hold her and love her, he wasn't sure where he'd find the patience to keep doing the backward-forward dance with her for months and months with no end in sight.

She might not be willing to admit or acknowledge she loved him, but he knew she did. It was evident in the way her eyes lit up every time she saw him. Love lingered in her smile when he called her beautiful, and it filled her voice when she said his name.

Before thoughts of her sent his blood firing through his veins this early in the morning, he avoided thinking about what her kisses did to him. Or the undeniable passion that pulsed between them each time her hand touched his. The rare, stolen moments they had alone together were made even sweeter when she'd wrap her arms around him and just want to hold him in a tight hug, as though she'd never had enough, would never get enough, of being close to him.

He tried to imagine what it would have been like to grow up without supportive, loving parents who offered words of praise or warm hugs, or comfort in those moments when he'd needed it most.

Sage had none of that growing up. It was no wonder she approached a relationship with him with a great deal of hesitancy. He knew Shane had abandonment issues he was working through, but he couldn't help but think Sage had a few of them, too.

Justin was pouring a bowl of cold cereal when he heard the crunch of gravel outside. He set down the box of cereal and stepped onto the deck as Shane jogged around the corner of the house with a big smile on his face.

"Hi, Justin!" the boy said as he took the steps two at a time.

"Did you have breakfast already?" Justin asked as Shane rushed inside the house.

"Yeah. Sage made pancakes and sausages and scrambled eggs this morning. She said if you haven't eaten yet and want some to let her know. She made extra." Shane looked at the box of sweetened cereal on the counter then shook his head. "You better call her, dude."

Justin watched as Shane stepped into the garage. He knew the boy would pet Crosby and retrieve the calf bottle and powdered milk replacer he mixed with water to feed Fred. While Shane fixed the calf's bottle Justin sent Sage a text.

Did you really make extra breakfast today?

Immediately, she replied back.

Yes, I did. Want some?

He sent another text.

Are you kidding? I'd crawl over there on my hands and knees for your fluffy, golden, deliciousness.

There was a pause before she responded.

Are we still talking about breakfast? My heart will be broken if you admit the only reason you keep me around is for pancakes and Bundt cake.

Justin grinned as he wrote a response and sent it.

I'd still crawl over there on my hands in knees even if you didn't know how to boil water. You are the most delicious thing I've ever tasted.

He could just picture her cheeks turning pink.

"Are you sending naughty messages to my sister?" Shane asked as he walked past him to feed the calf.

"I don't send those kinds of text messages, kid. Here's a lesson for you: Be a gentleman, even when you're texting. Besides, what I send her isn't any of your business." Justin gave Shane a playful shove out the patio door. "Don't you have a calf to feed?"

Shane laughed. "I sure do. I can hardly wait for this day to be over then I have three whole months free from school."

"Are you excited about working for Carson this summer?"

"It's gonna be great," Shane said, hurrying out to feed Fred. The calf started bawling and running toward the fence the moment he spied his breakfast in Shane's hands.

Justin turned his attention to the text message from Sage that popped up on his phone.

Breakfast? Yes or No?

He quickly fired off a reply.

Definitely yes.

She sent another text back

Here or HPH?

Matilda, Ruth, and the other residents at

Golden Skies would be offended if they ever discovered Justin, Sage, Fynlee, Carson, and a few others in their circle of friends referred to the retirement center as the Hokey Pokey Hotel. Sage abbreviated it to HPH to keep from giggling every time she said it. He'd seen her almost spill the beans one day when she'd been talking to Matilda and Fynlee mouthed it as she stood behind her grandmother.

Your place. I'll bring Shane home.

Justin put away the cereal, made his lunch, and chased Crosby out of the garage before he brushed his teeth and combed his hair. After making sure the front door was locked, he rinsed the calf bottle while Shane watered Fred and put fresh straw down in his enclosure.

When Shane finished, he walked around to the big garage door Justin had opened and loaded his bicycle in the back of the work truck, then climbed in the cab.

"Ready to go?" Justin asked as he backed up and pushed the button to close the garage door.

"Yep. I just need to change and grab my backpack." Shane looked out the window as Justin drove into town and made his way to Sage's little rental house. The house had a tiny living area, an even smaller kitchen, a bathroom Justin could barely turn around in, and two small bedrooms. Despite the cramped quarters, it was neat and clean, and in a section of town that was decent. It was also a place Sage could afford on her income.

Shane jumped out of the pickup the moment Justin parked at the curb and grabbed his bike. He leaned the bike against the front steps and ran inside while Justin made his way to the door. After a perfunctory knock, Justin stepped inside where he breathed in the pleasant aromas of breakfast mingling with Sage's delectable soft fragrance.

When she stuck her head around the doorway of the kitchen and smiled at him, his heart flip-flopped in his chest.

"Good morning," she said, giving him a warm smile and a kiss on his cheek when he stepped into the kitchen.

One good thing about her small house was that it didn't give her much room to sidle away from him. He slid his hands around her waist as she cracked two eggs into a skillet. She glanced over her shoulder at him and he brushed his mouth over hers.

"You taste like maple syrup," he mumbled against her lips.

"Is that good or bad?" she asked as she flipped over the eggs.

"Good." Justin wanted to forget about eggs and breakfast and Shane thumping around in his room as he got ready for school. He just wanted to spend the day holding Sage in his arms.

With his temperature rapidly rising and his resistance just as quickly ebbing, he pressed a kiss to Sage's neck and stepped back. The look she gave him kicked his internal thermostat up several notches. He took another step back away from the temptation of the gorgeous woman frying eggs.

Sage wore a navy skirt with a soft summery blouse that accented her golden hair and creamy skin. No matter what she wore, Justin always thought she looked lovely, but something about the buttery-yellow top she wore and the fact she'd left her hair hanging in long curls made him wish he could start every day with her.

"How come you made extra food for breakfast this morning?" he asked. He took the plate she handed him with the eggs cooked just the way he liked, a stack of pancakes, and three sausage patties. Carefully pulling out a chair at the tiny table in the corner of the kitchen, he sat down and drizzled syrup over the pancakes. He nodded with thanks when she set a glass of milk in front of him.

"I wasn't thinking when I mixed the pancake batter and made a full batch instead of half like I usually do. I decided I might as well cook a few extra sausages and see if I could find some handsome hunk to come share the food with me." Sage sat beside him and took a sip from a cup of tea she held with both hands.

Justin raised his eyebrows in question. "Did you have a particular hunk in mind, or would you have let just any handsome guy in here?"

"Well…" Sage pretended to consider the question for a long moment before she grinned at him and nudged his arm with her shoulder. "You know you're the only guy that comes around here, unless you count Shane."

"Count me for what?" the teen asked as he raced into the room. He wore cargo shorts, a T-shirt with his school logo emblazoned across the front, and sneakers that weren't fully tied. His shaggy hair had been combed into some semblance of order.

Justin had offered to take him to the barbershop weeks ago, but Shane had informed him he was letting his hair grow out for a while. Apparently, a girl he liked had commented how much she liked a certain movie star who sported longer hair. Sage had told him as long as he didn't plan on letting it grow as long as hers, she'd let him get away with it for a while.

"Breakfast," Justin said, holding up a bite of pancakes on his fork.

Shane grinned. "I'm stuffed." He hugged Sage around her neck and grabbed the sack lunch she'd left for him on the end of the counter. With a wave, he raced toward the front door. "I'm gonna ride my bike to school. See you later!"

"Helmet, Shane! Don't forget your helmet!"

The boy's sigh carried back into the kitchen but Justin leaned to the side far enough he could see Shane tug on the helmet before he raced off.

"I think you have eyes in the back of your head, hiding beneath all that incredible hair." Justin lifted his hand and let it glide over her glossy curls. "I don't feel anything, but I'm sure they are there."

"You're crazy," she said with a grin, then motioned to his plate. "Eat your breakfast or we'll both be late for work."

"Do you miss me being at the Hokey Pokey Hotel every day?"

Sage cast him a flirty grin. "Why would I miss you with all the dapper gentlemen there? They flirt and flatter and make me feel like a princess."

"You might miss me because I still have my own teeth and don't require a walker to get around or smell like pain-relieving rub." He narrowed his gaze. "Maybe you're some kind of weirdo into the geriatric set, in which case I don't want to know."

She scowled at him and grabbed his plate, playfully tugging it away from him. "If you're going to be ornery, no more breakfast for you."

"Hey, leave my pancakes alone," he said, pulling the plate back in front of him and hovering over it.

Sage giggled and finished her tea. "I'll be back in a minute. Do you need anything else?" she asked as she rose to her feet.

"No, Beautiful. Breakfast is tasty." He took her hand, turned it over, and pressed a moist kiss to her palm. When she shivered in response, he gazed up at her with a rascally grin. "But not quite as delectable as you."

"You better just save that for another time, Romeo," Sage said, yanking her hand away. Her eyes held a mixture of warning and yearning when she looked at him. "Behave."

Justin winked at her. "I've already told you, there is no fun to be had in that."

"Which is exactly why you should behave." She gave him another warning glance then rushed from the room.

Justin finished his breakfast, and washed his dishes and the skillet she'd left on the stove after cooking his eggs. He grabbed a dishrag and wiped off the stove and table. He was drying his hands when she returned to the kitchen wearing a pair of high heels that drew his attention to the attractive shape of her legs visible beneath the knee-length hem of her skirt. Her fresh, floral scent floated around him. He swallowed a groan and shoved his hands into his pockets to keep from taking her in his arms and never letting go.

Sage looked around the kitchen then turned to him with a grateful smile. "You really would make someone a wonderful wife."

He chuckled and grabbed for her, making her squeal as she hurried toward the front door. Justin caught her before she could pull it open and wrapped his arms around her. "That's not a compliment, Sage. In fact, it's rather emasculating."

"I just meant you're handy to have around." She stopped squirming and turned around to face him, slipping her arms around his neck.

With her heels on, Justin didn't have to bend far to capture her lips in a sweet kiss.

Her eyelashes fluttered against her cheeks when he pulled back, as though she savored the kiss, the tender moment. "I better get going."

"Me, too. My first appointment is a few miles out of town." Justin walked outside with Sage and watched as she locked the door and pulled it shut. "Want to have lunch today?"

She glanced up at him in pleased surprise. "I'd love that. Do you want me to meet you somewhere?"

"No, I'll pick you up. Does noon work?" he asked as he walked her over to her car and held the door while she got in and buckled her seatbelt.

"That's perfect. See you then."

He bent down and gave her a brief parting kiss. "Thanks for breakfast. It really was good."

"You're welcome."

Justin shut her door and watched her back onto the street. She gave him a parting wave before she drove away.

The morning passed quickly and he soon found himself brushing dirt off the front of his shirt and work pants and stamping dust off his boots as he strolled down the walk to the lobby at Golden Skies.

When he stepped inside, a good-looking muscular man ran his hand along one of Sage's long curls and brushed it back from her shoulder as he smiled at her.

She laughed at something the man said and leaned back in her chair. The man sat down on the corner of her desk, as though he planned to stay for a while.

Every primitive, cavedweller-like instinct Justin possessed roared to the surface, begging to knock the guy off the desk and onto the floor.

By sheer will, Justin somehow refrained from the urge to deck the man as he walked up to Sage's desk.

"Hi, Justin." Sage greeted him with a welcoming smile as she rose to her feet. "This is Dr. Dawson. He's one of the physicians Golden Skies recently hired." She glanced from Justin to the doctor. "Justin James is the electrician who worked on the new wing."

"Nice to meet you," the doctor said, holding out his hand.

Reluctantly, Justin took it and shook the man's

hand then looked to Sage. "Are you ready to go to lunch?"

"I am," she said, picking up her purse and slipping the straps over her shoulder before smiling at the doctor. "Thanks for your help."

"Anytime," the doctor said, eyeing Sage with interest. "Enjoy your lunch and the sunshine. It's sure a pretty day."

Justin had an idea what the doctor found pretty was Sage, not the flowers blooming in profusion outside. He scowled as he escorted Sage out to his pickup and helped her inside. It wasn't until he slid behind the wheel that he turned and stared at her.

"What's wrong?" she asked, reaching out to touch his hand. He jerked back before she could touch it.

He gave her a hard glare. "Why was the good doctor running his hands through your hair?"

The expression on her face appeared baffled. "My hair?"

"When I walked in, he was stroking your hair."

Sage rolled her eyes and released an exasperated breath. "If you must know, Matilda and Ruth were outside in the courtyard and were convinced they saw a baby bunny in the bushes. They asked me to come out and look beneath a rhododendron to see if I could find it. There was no bunny, but I did find a cranky squirrel and ended up with cobwebs in my hair. Dr. Dawson was brushing out one I missed." She gave him a curious glance. "You aren't jealous are you?"

Justin started the pickup and backed out of the parking space. "Maybe, a little."

"Wow. So this is what it feels like," she said, grinning at him.

"What feels like?" he asked, confused and embarrassed he'd made a big deal out of such a little thing.

"Having a boy like me enough another one made him jealous." She batted her eyelashes at him and made an exaggerated kissy face.

Justin chuckled and shook his head. "First of all, I'm not a boy."

"Then don't act like one," she countered, raising her eyebrow for emphasis.

"Point taken." He gave her a long look. "How would you feel if you saw a woman running her hands through my hair?"

Sage appeared to consider his words for a moment then mumbled something he couldn't hear.

"What did you say?"

"Never mind. How about we change the subject?" she asked as he pulled into the parking lot at the café.

"Fine with me," he said, hurrying out of the pickup to open her door.

It wasn't until they were driving back to Golden Skies that Justin felt the need to broach a subject he'd been avoiding. "Sage, you have to know by now how much I enjoy being with you. Honestly, you make every day so much better just by being in it. I realize we haven't spent much time alone or done much in the way of dating, unless you want to count our Friday night dinners chaperoned by Shane, but I'm crazy about you. I love you, Sage, and I hope we have a shot at building something wonderful together."

Rather than the look of love he'd hoped to see on her face, she appeared completely panic-stricken.

"Sage, what is it?" he asked, taking her hand in his and bringing it to his lips. He pressed a soft kiss to the back of her hand and waited for her to speak.

"I care about you, too, Justin. More than I should," she said, slowly pulling her hand away from his grasp. "I like being with you and enjoy our friendship, but there can't ever be more. Do you understand what I'm trying to say?"

"No, not at all," Justin said, whipping into a parking space at Golden Skies. He threw the pickup into park and turned in the seat to stare at her. "Are you saying you don't want to see me anymore?"

"Yes. No. I don't..." Sage sighed and covered her face with both hands before she took a deep breath and faced him. "You are an amazing, wonderful, kind, funny, incredible man, Justin. You deserve far, far more than I could ever give you. Regardless of how I feel about you or what I wish could happen, our relationship is never going to move beyond the casual dating stage. Shane has been and will continue to be my top priority. It isn't fair to anyone for me to pretend otherwise."

"But, Sage, you don't have to..."

"No, Justin. Please don't make this harder." Her fingers covered his lips as she shook her head. "Perhaps it's best if we take a break for a while. Maybe the summer will give us time to see things with a little clarity." She slid back across the cab and opened her door. "Thank you for everything you've done for me, for us. I appreciate you more than you'll ever know."

Before he could say anything, she scrambled out of the pickup and raced inside Golden Skies. He watched her go, confused, with an aching hole in his heart.

Chapter Ten

Justin couldn't wait to get home, kick off his boots, and collapse in his recliner with the pizza sitting on the passenger seat of his pickup. The smell of meat and spices made his stomach growl, reminding him he'd missed lunch.

From the moment he got up that morning and found Fred Asteer standing in the flower beds, the day hadn't gone well.

Truthfully, he'd felt like he'd been living in a fog since Sage said it was best they took a break and didn't see each other for a while. He had no idea if she planned to ignore him all summer or for eternity. He'd tried texting and calling her, but she didn't answer or respond to his messages.

Although he hated it, he knew he had to give her the space she'd requested. If she'd just talk to him instead of pushing him away, she'd know that he had no intention of taking Shane's place. Justin didn't expect her to ignore her brother just because he wanted to spend time with her, too. For the most part, he didn't mind Shane being with them. The boy's presence had proved to be a challenge for his patience on a few occasions when Justin had wanted nothing more than to ravish Sage with kisses, but Shane made a great chaperone.

In hindsight, a few stolen kisses when Shane wasn't looking were far better than none at all.

Honestly, Justin had enjoyed hanging out with Sage and Shane. He often held her hand as they watched a movie on TV or they went for walks. Sometimes she wrapped her arms around his waist and just leaned into him, like she had a deficit of hugs and needed to fill the void.

Each and every time they touched, whether by accident or intent, it made Justin feel things he'd never experienced before, never dreamed of feeling.

He knew Sage wasn't perfect. The woman was stubborn and independent, emotionally withdrawn on occasion, and fearful of relationships. None of that was a secret to him. But it didn't change his opinion that she was perfect for him. She made him laugh and think, made him want to be a better version of himself, made him grateful and happy. So incredibly happy.

The love he felt for her was all-consuming, passionate, selfless, and tender. He wanted to love her wholly, completely, unreservedly. Until she realized a relationship with him didn't mean she had to exclude Shane, there wasn't anything Justin could say or do to change her mind.

Frustrated and weary, Justin drove around his house and into the garage. After parking the pickup, he closed the garage door and carried the pizza into the kitchen. He glanced out the patio door to see Fred standing on the deck munching on a weed that grew abundantly along the road.

That crazy calf was going to get himself killed if he was playing in the road. Shane had told him just that morning that Sage decided it would be better if Fred was back at the Flying B Ranch. Shane was spending most of his time there anyway.

Since the end of school, Shane had been working for Carson. One of the ranch hands who lived in town drove him out each morning and Sage picked him up each evening. But Shane faithfully came over twice a day to feed and water Fred. Now that the calf was no longer on a bottle, Justin could have easily fed the calf his grain and filled his water tank, but Shane seemed to enjoy coming over in the morning and again each evening.

Justin hated to admit how much he enjoyed those quick visits with Shane. The boy had grown an inch and his recently-cut hair was getting lighter while his skin turned darker from all the time he spent out in the sun at the ranch. Carson had given him a pair of his uncle's old boots that Shane proudly wore everywhere.

If Shane took Fred back to the ranch, Justin would never get to see him, or Sage.

Matilda and Ruth had been in fine form once they realized Sage had put a stop to their budding romance. Rather than building a future based on hope, love and trust, Justin was left alone, trying to figure out exactly where things had gone so wrong.

In an effort to reconcile him with Sage, the two old women had invented half a dozen reasons for him to come to Golden Skies. It would have taken a blind fool to not see through their schemes, but Justin went along with each one because he'd wanted — needed — to see Sage. She'd been cordial, but not overly friendly when he was there to test an outlet or check a light socket for Ruth and Matilda.

The two conniving matchmakers did their best until Sage told them if they called him for no reason again, she would make sure they both got prune juice in their morning coffee.

Regrettably, he hadn't received a call from them in more than a week.

Evidently prune juice trumped true love.

Justin opened the patio door and slid his fingers around Fred's halter that he'd given Shane for Easter. The calf didn't seem to mind wearing it and it sure made catching him easier when he got out, which was happening with increasing frequency the past few days. Justin didn't know why Fred wouldn't stay in his pen or even where he was getting out.

If Shane hadn't mentioned moving him back to the Flying B, Justin had planned to spend time that weekend adding hog wire along the lower half of the fence. He had an idea Fred just rolled under the bottom of it and went on his merry way.

"Come on, Fred." Justin pulled the weed out of the calf's mouth and tossed it aside. "Shane will be here soon and you know he worries when you're not where you're supposed to be." He led the calf over to the gate and gave him a nudge inside the pasture.

Crosby followed them and meowed, then rubbed against Fred's legs.

Justin didn't want to think about what Crosby would do if his new friend left. Other than Fred, Sage and Shane, Crosby tolerated Justin, but stayed far away from all other living, breathing things.

"Let's get you fed, Crosby, so I can eat my dinner before it tastes like cold cardboard."

Justin closed the gate and made his way back to the house. He fed and watered Crosby, then unbuttoned his shirt and left it in the laundry room before returning to the kitchen and washing his hands, face, and arms.

He'd just toweled off when he glanced outside and saw Shane feeding Fred and making sure the calf had fresh water. Justin would have done it when he was out there, but Shane insisted on taking care of the calf himself.

Two long strides carried him across the kitchen and to the patio door. He pulled it open and wondered if the evening would cool off or stay unbearably hot. It was only the first full week of June and seemed unseasonably warm to him.

"Hey, Shane, want to eat pizza with me?" he called as the boy rolled up the hose and brushed his hands on the seat of his jeans.

"Sure! That sounds great," Shane said, hurrying across the backyard and up the steps to the deck.

"How's it going?" Justin asked. He moved back as Shane wiped his boots on the doormat then stepped inside and closed the patio door. The cool air blowing around them felt refreshing after being out in the heat most of the day.

"Good. I really like working at the Flying B. I'm learning a lot about cattle and horses and ranching and farming." Shane washed his hands at the sink then took a seat at the table where Justin had set two plates, the box of pizza, and two glasses of Dr Pepper.

Justin opened the box and set two pieces of pizza on each plate then handed one to Shane. "Do you need to let your sister know you're eating dinner here?"

"Nah. She knows where I am and she said we're having salad for dinner because it's so hot out and she didn't want to heat up the house by cooking anything." Shane bit into his pizza and grinned. "I'll eat the salad, but I'm hungry after a day at the ranch."

Justin grinned. "I imagine a growing boy like you needs more than a salad for dinner."

"Oh, she puts meat and cheese on it, but I have to eat two bowls full to keep my stomach from growling." Shane took another bite of his pizza then gulped his soda. "Did Fred get out again?"

"He was out when I got home."

Shane gave him a worried glance. "I'm sorry. I guess it really is best to move him this weekend. Carson has a small pen near the house where I can keep him, but it's just dirt, not grass. I wish I could leave him here."

"Can you talk to Sage, let her know you want to keep him here?"

A sigh rolled out of Shane. "I've tried talking to her about it, but she refuses to listen." The boy looked at him for a long moment then set down his pizza. "If I did something to mess things up between the two of you, I'm sorry. I kinda hoped... well, I just thought that you... that Sage..."

Justin reached over and placed his hand on Shane's shoulder, giving it a squeeze. "It's okay, Shane. You didn't do anything wrong. What's going on between your sister and me doesn't have anything to do with you. Got it?"

"Got it," Shane said, appearing relieved as he took another bite from his pizza.

They were both on their third piece when Crosby began yowling loudly from the garage. Justin got up and opened the door. The cat raced to the patio door. He pawed at it, meowing demandingly as Justin opened it.

"Did Crosby get into some loco weed?" Shane asked as he moved beside Justin at the patio door and observed the cat.

They watched Crosby scamper across the yard and into the pasture where Fred listed from one side to the other, like he was drunk.

"That can't be good," Justin said, racing across the deck, down the steps, and to the pasture with Shane right behind him. He jumped over the fence and rushed to Fred. The calf had a yellowish discharge running from his nose and eyes, and bawled pitifully as he staggered around.

"What's wrong with him?" Shane asked as he reached out and wrapped his arms around the calf.

Fred nuzzled against him, smearing the sticky

discharge from his nose all over Shane's shirt.

"I'm not sure," Justin said, looking up the number of the local vet and placing a call. He spoke to the vet, who promised to be there as soon as he could, then disconnected the call.

"Let's get him in the shade," Justin said, picking up the calf and carrying him out of the pasture. When he reached the back yard, he settled the calf in the cool grass beneath one of the big shade trees.

Shane sat beside the calf and placed Fred's head on his lap where he could stroke it.

Justin filled a bucket with water and drizzled some over Fred's nose, hoping to get him to take a drink.

The calf bawled again and panted hard, as though he struggled to draw in a breath.

Justin cupped water in his hand and held it against Fred's lips. The calf took a little of the cool liquid, but immediately went back to panting. His little sides heaved and he appeared listless as Justin continued to try to get him to drink.

Minutes passed in what seemed like hours as they waited for the vet. Shane was practically beside himself with worry as he clung to Fred and pleaded with him to be okay.

Justin's heart ached for the boy. He knew the calf was more than just a 4-H project to him. It was his beloved pet, a friend, and one more being he loved that might abandon him. The last thing the boy needed was another loss in his young life.

He placed a hand on Shane's back and rubbed it comfortingly as he sent up a prayer for God to spare the calf for the boy's sake. Involved in his worries about Shane and the calf, he didn't hear a car approach and jumped when a hand touched his arm.

When Sage found her brother, he was going to get a lecture he wouldn't soon forget. Shane was supposed to feed Fred then come straight home. She knew he liked to visit with Justin, but after Carson moved the calf back to the Flying B on Saturday, there would be no reason for her brother to bother the electrician again.

Shane had begged and pleaded with her to leave Fred at Justin's place, but she couldn't stand the thought of being beholden to him more than she already was. Since she'd declared her need for space from him and their relationship, she couldn't very well make him dinner on Fridays as payment for rent.

She hadn't even thought about what she'd do to pay Carson for keeping the calf. He and Fynlee had already done so much for her and Shane. When Carson suggested Shane work on the ranch for the summer, Sage had wanted to weep with relief. She had no idea what to do with her brother once school released at the end of May. The previous year, he'd slept until noon, wanted to play video games half the night, and was bored to tears while she worked.

Shane needed to keep busy and he loved being out at the ranch. Almost as much as he loved hanging out with Justin.

Why, oh why, had she ignored what her head was telling her and allowed her heart to call the shots where handsome Justin James was concerned. She knew it was foolish to agree to date him, no matter how much she wanted to.

She'd enjoyed every minute she'd spent with him. He was funny and clever, smart and strong, kind and gentle. There wasn't a single thing about him she'd change even if she could. Justin was everything she could hope for in a man, everything she wanted in a husband, but dreams of marriage weren't meant for a girl who had a teenage boy to raise.

Now that she'd cracked the door to her heart and let Justin toe his way inside, she didn't know how she'd ever get past the longing and love she felt for him. While she freely admitted she was attracted to the good-looking man, it was so much more than that. Justin made her feel safe and cherished. He made her believe her dreams could come true. And he made her want to love him without reserve or restraint, but with her whole heart. Only, she couldn't. Not when loving someone meant they'd eventually leave her. The last thing she'd allow was Shane to lose one more person he cared about.

Tumultuous thoughts swirled through her head as she tried to get in touch with Shane. As upset as she was with her brother for not answering her texts or returning the voice messages she left, she might ground him until he left for college.

While Shane had gone to take care of Fred,

Sage had exchanged her work skirt and blouse for a pair of shorts and a tank top, then made steak salads for dinner. Shane whined that a working man needed more sustenance, so she'd cooked twice the amount of meat.

It should have only taken her brother twenty minutes at the most to ride to Justin's house, feed the calf, and return home.

When twenty minutes stretched to thirty, her anger began simmering. By the time an hour had passed, she was furious with both Shane and Justin. As a so-called responsible adult, Justin should have known she'd be worried about Shane and sent him home. She could just picture the two of them sitting at Justin's table eating pizza or ice cream.

Angry and concerned, she shoved her feet into a pair of sandals, grabbed her purse, and marched outside. The heat nearly suffocated her as she rushed toward her car. She flinched as she scooted into the car and bare skin connected with the hot seat. Her clothes stuck to her as though they'd been plastered to her body as she waited for the air conditioner to kick on and bring welcome coolness.

She drove to Justin's place and parked out front next to where Shane had left his bicycle leaning against the front gate. Without giving it a conscious thought, she fluffed her hair and pinched her cheeks before she got out of the car and hurried up the walk.

No one answered the doorbell when she rang it, so she walked around the side of the house. In the backyard, Shane and Justin bent over a sickly-looking Fred while the cat sat nearby, keeping an eye on them all. It looked as though Justin was praying as he rested a comforting hand on her brother's back.

Shocked and uncertain what to do, Sage touched Justin's arm and sank down beside him. "What's wrong with him?"

"I'm not sure, but I think he might have eaten something he shouldn't have," Justin said in a quiet voice as Shane looked up at Sage with tears in his eyes.

"He can't die, Sage. He just can't." Shane shot her a pleading look, as though she could magically fix what was wrong.

Sage had learned a long time ago not to make promises she couldn't keep. She had no control over whether Fred would live or die, but it wouldn't stop her from trying to keep him alive.

"Does he need water? The vet? What can I do?" she asked Justin.

"The vet is on his way and we've been trying to get Fred to drink." Justin took her hand in his and gave it a squeeze.

In the weeks since she'd pushed him away she'd missed his touch, missed the comfort and security she felt with him, missed the warmth of his presence, and the peace of knowing he cared for her.

She watched as Justin worked with the calf while comforting Shane. He encouraged her brother, but didn't offer him false hope either. Justin was so good with him, so patient and kind. Someday, he'd make a wonderful father because he'd been an amazing father-figure to Shane.

The vet arrived and Sage moved back while Shane stayed close to Justin.

When the man she loved dropped an arm around the boy she adored, the truth hit her with such force, she had to turn away and take a gasping breath. Justin would do what was best for Shane. He hadn't abandoned her brother when she arrived, even though she knew he wanted to talk to her. He'd focused his whole attention on helping Shane with Fred.

While most men wouldn't want to be saddled with a teenager to raise, Justin would never look at Shane as a burden. He'd as much as said he knew she and Shane were a package deal, but until that moment, she hadn't realized he'd meant it.

Justin had offered her his love and she'd tossed it back to him, too afraid to accept it, too fearful to hope for a future with him. She hadn't wanted to think there was even a slight possibility for her to reach out and grasp happiness with Justin.

She could no longer deny the truth. Not only could she trust him with her heart, she could also trust him with Shane. But now wasn't the time to say anything.

The vet asked Justin questions, then answered the questions Shane asked. Justin pointed to something near the deck and Shane ran over to grab it and brought it back. The vet nodded his head at the sight of the half-eaten weed.

"Too many of those weeds can kill livestock," the vet said. "He should be fine once they work through his system, just make sure he doesn't eat any more of them."

"Thank you, sir," Shane said, dropping down beside Fred and rubbing his hand over the calf's neck.

Justin straightened and shook the vet's hand. "I appreciate you coming out like this."

"No problem," the vet said, grinning at Justin. "I take it you were in the middle of something when you noticed the calf was sick."

Justin glanced down, as though he just remembered he'd taken his shirt off earlier. He rubbed his hand over his chest and Sage's eyes followed every move.

Awareness and tension pulsed between them like a palpable force, but Justin seemed to shrug it off as he walked the vet out front.

Sage knelt in the grass and placed a hand on Shane's arm. He looked over at her and smiled. "He's going to be fine, Sage. Isn't that great news?"

"It is great news." She patted her brother then picked up Crosby when the cat pushed against her, demanding attention.

Crosby started to purr. Fred turned his head and nosed the cat and let out a huff of air that sounded like a relieved sigh.

"Do I really have to move him back to the ranch?" Shane asked as he continued to stroke Fred's neck.

"No. If Justin doesn't mind, you can keep him here. Although I think we better figure out a way to keep Fred inside the pasture so this doesn't happen again."

Shane grinned. "Justin said we need to put up hog wire along the bottom of the fence to keep Fred from escaping. He said I can help him do it, if it's okay with you."

Sage nodded. "It's okay with me. Do you think I might be able to help, too?"

Shane's head snapped up and he stared at her. "Really? You'd help and spend time around Justin. I thought you were mad at him or something."

"I'm not mad at him. Not at all. I just needed to figure out a few things." Sage continued petting the cat, mindful of the reality of her words. She'd needed time to realize how precious Justin was to her, how much she wanted and needed him in her life — in Shane's life, too. She hadn't expected it, hadn't looked for it, but she'd found her knight in shining armor. Only he wore work boots and could twist conduit into unbelievable works of art.

"Justin is one of the nicest, most genuine guys I've ever met. He's been a good friend to us both and I care about him a great deal."

"Do you love him?" Shane asked, giving her a curious glance.

Slowly, Sage's head worked up and down. "I do. Does that bother you?"

"Heck, no! Justin's cool." Shane dribbled water over Fred's nose. "Does that mean we can have dinner together on Friday nights again?"

"If Justin wants to we can."

Shane gave her an impish grin. "Are you gonna let him kiss you again?"

She scowled at her brother, but before she could reply to his question, strong hands clasped her upper arms and pulled her to her feet.

Justin offered her a cocky smile as he took the

cat from her, setting Crosby on the grass. He wrapped his arms around her and looked at her with an intensity that made her legs quiver.

"You didn't answer Shane's question," Justin said, continuing to hold her gaze. "Are you gonna let me kiss you again?"

Heat soaked her cheeks, staining them bright pink. She wanted to fidget, to duck her head, to hide. But she didn't. She looked into his warm brown eyes brimming with love and smiled. "How long were you standing behind me?"

"Long enough to know you're in love with me and are ready to resume our Friday date nights." Justin pulled her a little closer.

Sage loved the feel of being in his arms, especially without his shirt in the way to hamper her ability to trail her fingers across his warm, tanned skin. She skimmed her fingers over his chest then entwined them in the hair at the back of his neck.

"You still haven't answered Shane's very important question," Justin said, drawing her so close, Sage could see sparks firing in the depths of his mesmerizing eyes.

Rather than speak, she bracketed Justin's face in her hands and pressed her lips to his. Justin lifted her off her feet and deepened the kiss as longing and promises for tomorrow encircled them in a glorious place where nothing else existed.

Snickers finally drew them back to reality. She and Justin turned as Shane watched them. "Am I gonna have to get used to seeing that all the time?"

"That depends," Justin said, kissing Sage on the nose before he set her back on her feet.

"On what?" Shane asked.

"On if you and your sister will come live here with me."

Shane cheered with excitement as Justin picked a flower from a nearby flower bed, then dropped to his knee. He took Sage's hand in his and kissed the back of it, then held up the single daisy stem. "I don't have a ring, but I love you Sage Presley, with all my heart. You and Shane, both. Would you do me the honor of becoming my wife and giving me the little brother I've always wanted?"

"She will!" Shane shouted.

Sage tossed a squelching scowl at Shane then turned to Justin, tugging on his hand until he stood. "I would be the one honored to marry you, Justin. I love you with all my heart and I have since the moment you set foot in Golden Skies. Nothing would please me more than becoming your bride."

Justin swept her into his arms and swung her around while Shane whooped excitedly. "When are you going to get married?" the boy asked when Justin finally set Sage back on her feet.

Sage glanced at Justin then at her brother. "I always thought it would be wonderful to be a summer bride."

"Then that's what you'll be," Justin said. He kissed her again and she knew life would never be the same. From that moment on, it would be so much better, so much richer, and so full of love.

Chapter Eleven

"Stand still," Justin's sister warned as she attempted to straighten his tie. She had to stretch to reach him with the mound of her pregnant belly between them.

Justin grinned as the baby kicked and he felt the jolt against his side. "He's gonna be a football star, Janie."

She scowled at him as she finished with his tie then brushed a speck of lint from the lapel of his tux. "Your niece can play football if she wishes, but I'd rather see her be a ballerina."

He kissed his sister's cheek. "Mom still hasn't talked you into finding out if it's a boy or a girl?"

"No, she hasn't. Brad and I want to be surprised." Janie stepped back and gave him a critical once-over. "You'll do."

"That's a relief. I thought maybe I was a don't

and then what would happen?" Justin teased, drawing a snort from his brother-in-law.

Janie frowned at her husband. "The two of you are impossible. I'm going to go check on Sage."

"Hey, would you give her this? Please?" Justin took a small envelope from his pocket and handed it to her.

Janie offered him an indulgent smile. "Of course." She took a step back and looked around the courtyard at Golden Skies. "I can't believe you're getting married at a retirement village."

"Sage and I thought about getting married at my place, but the residents here would have been so disappointed if they couldn't attend since they all love Sage." Justin watched as Matilda Dale pranced into the courtyard wearing a flowing dress bedecked with sequined sunflowers. Ruth Beaumont followed her, looking like she stepped off a southern veranda in a lilac-colored dress with a wide white straw hat. The two women headed toward them, beaming from ear to ear.

"Justin, you look quite dashing," Matilda said in a loud voice that drew gazes their way.

"Thank you, Matilda. You and Ruth both look ready for a party." He grinned at the two older women. "You met my sister, didn't you?"

"We certainly did," Ruth said, smiling at Janie. "Would you like to come inside out of the heat, dear? The ceremony will begin soon, but no need to stand out here melting in the sun when you don't need to."

"I was just on my way inside to check on Sage. Would you like to accompany me?" Janie asked, holding out a hand to Ruth.

The older woman took it while Matilda flanked her other side.

Justin watched them go, amazed that an electrical job resulted in him finding the woman who completed him. Sage enriched his life in ways he could barely comprehend, let alone articulate. He loved her and Shane, and couldn't wait to have them both living at his house, sharing in his life.

It seemed perfect Sage had asked if they could wed on the first day of summer. Justin had no objection to marrying quickly rather than dragging it out. He'd known for months Sage was the one he was meant to love forever. Nothing was going to change that.

"The pastor looks like he's ready to get things rolling. Should we head over there?" Brad asked, drawing Justin from his thoughts.

He nodded and the two of them walked to a bower of daisies that had been erected at one end of the courtyard. Justin had no idea how they'd pulled it off, but under Ruth and Matilda's guidance, the courtyard had been transformed into an incredible summer garden with enough lights and flowers to leave even the pickiest bride in awe. Balls of daisies hung from buttery yellow ribbons on the end of each row of white chairs. An aisle with a white runner led from the doorway into the courtyard and up to the bower where Justin waited with Brad.

Everywhere he looked there were more flowers, in baskets and buckets and vases. Most of the flowers were daisies, but others were included in the mix, too. The courtyard truly looked amazing and he knew Sage was thrilled with the results. At least she sounded excited in the many texts they'd exchanged that morning.

"Are we ready?" Carson asked as he stepped beside Brad, taking his place as Justin's groomsman.

"I think we are," Justin said, eager for the wedding to begin so he could move on to his happily ever after with his beautiful bride.

Carson caught Fynlee's eye where she waited by the door and motioned to her. She stepped inside and soon residents poured out and filled the seats.

Sage had no family, other than the residents, but Justin's parents, cousins, and aunts and uncles had all come for the wedding. He was surprised so many of them made the trip, but then again, he'd gone to all of their graduations, weddings, and special events. He just hoped they didn't overwhelm Sage.

Ruth and Matilda took seats in the front row along with Rand. An usher seated Justin's parents next to them. Soft classical music played as Janie waddled down the aisle holding a bouquet of daisies in front of her rounded belly. Fynlee walked behind her, also carrying a bouquet of daisies.

Justin smiled as the wedding march began and Sage stepped outside on Shane's arm. He grinned at them both as they made their way up the aisle to him.

When the minister asked who gave Sage in marriage, Shane spoke up and said, "I do, sir."

Justin winked at the boy as he took Sage's hand in his and turned to face the minister. Shane took a seat between Ruth and Justin's mother, looking as though he might bust the buttons right off his starched white shirt.

"Thank you for the note," Sage whispered before the pastor continued with the ceremony.

"I meant every word," Justin said, leaning so close his lips brushed her ear. She'd left her hair down, hanging in golden coils beneath her filmy veil. The sleeveless lace gown she wore was classic and tasteful, and so perfect for Sage. She carried a bouquet of daisies, but mixed among the flowers were little sprigs of sage that scented the air around them.

"I should hope so since there were only five of them," she said in a low tone only he could hear. "My heart is yours forever, too."

Justin squeezed her hand as the pastor began the ceremony. When it was time to exchange rings, Sage's hand trembled slightly as Justin slipped a vintage Art Deco-style platinum ring on her finger. She presented him with a ring made entirely of wood, "because the only jolts I want you to get are from our kisses," she said as she slipped the ring on his hand.

The pastor chuckled and finished the ceremony by pronouncing them husband and wife. With enthusiasm, he encouraged Justin to kiss his bride.

He lifted her veil, wrapped his arms around her, and gave her a kiss that held just enough passion to let her know she was wanted, and a measure of tenderness to assure her she was cherished.

When he lifted his head, he bent back down and kissed her cheek then looked to the pastor.

"Shane, please join us," the pastor said, motioning for the boy to come up to the bower. Shane shot them a confused look, but stood and walked over to where they waited.

Justin took another ring from his pocket and handed it to Sage. She studied it then smiled at him before looking at the pastor.

The man nodded and cleared his throat. "Justin wanted it known and witnessed by each of you that today he has not only given his heart and love to Sage, promising to cherish and protect her, but his love and protection extends to Shane as well. Sage, please slide the ring onto your brother's finger."

Sage took Shane's right hand and slid on the ring, then looked to Justin. He placed his hands over both of theirs, holding them all together. "This is a unity ring. You'll see it's two individual strands that have been woven together. That's what we'll be." Justin smiled at Shane "You are your own person, Shane, but you'll always be family to Sage and to me."

Shane swallowed hard and hugged Sage then accepted the bear hug Justin gave him.

"Now, it's my pleasure to introduce for the first time the newly formed James family!" the pastor said in a loud, cheerful voice.

Justin led Sage down the aisle while Shane followed behind them with the bridal party. They assembled in the Golden Skies recreation room that had been transformed into an incredible reception area.

Sage took Shane's hand in hers and studied the ring, then threw her arms around Justin's neck.

"Thank you for including Shane in the ceremony."

"Yeah, man, thank you for this cool ring." Shane toyed with the band on his finger then kissed Sage's cheek. "I'm proud to be part of your family. In fact, I'm gonna go find my new grandma because she promised to tell me stories about stupid things you did at my age."

Justin rolled his eyes and grinned as Shane hurried over to where Janie, Brad, and some of Justin's relatives visited.

"That was such an amazing thing for you to do, Justin," Sage said, giving him another hug. "I can't believe I'm married to such a wonderful guy."

"Well, you better believe it, Beautiful, because I'm not going anywhere." Justin wrapped his arms around her waist and pulled her close. "You and Shane are stuck with me for a long, long time."

"I'm glad." Sage kissed his cheek then stepped back and wrapped her hand around his arm so they could watch their friends and family. "It was nice of your family to offer to take Shane with them to the lake for the weekend so we could enjoy a few days to ourselves."

"I'm counting the minutes until we can sneak out of this party and get started on more interesting endeavors."

Sage gave him an indulgent smile, one full of acceptance and love. "If it helps, the wedding cake is my lemon Bundt cake recipe."

"That does help," Justin said, kissing her neck and pulling her close against him once more. "I love you so much, Sage. I promise to do my best to show you just how much you are loved every single day."

"And I promise to do my best to show you how much I love you, cherish you, and want you every single day." She turned around so she faced him. Her fingers trailed along his jaw and she looked at him with her heart dancing in her eyes. "You are the best thing that's ever happened to me, Justin James, and I look forward to spending the rest of my life loving you. Thank you for your love and for giving me and Shane a place to call home, in your heart."

Keep reading for a preview from Easter Bride, the next book in the Holiday Brides series.

Recipe

I've said it before, but I'll admit it again — I am a Bundt cake junkie. I love, love, love Bundt cake recipes. This one is perfect for spring or summer gatherings — or any time you want a burst of delicious lemony-flavor. Enjoy!

Lemon Bundt Cake

1 box white or lemon cake mix
1 small package instant lemon pudding
1 cup sour cream
1/2 cup water
1/2 cup oil
3 eggs
1 tsp. lemon juice
2/3 cup cream cheese frosting
1 fresh lemon (optional)
Strawberries (optional)

Preheat oven to 350 degrees.

Lightly beat eggs. Blend with cake mix, oil, sour cream, water and lemon juice on medium speed until combined. The batter should be relatively thick, so don't worry if it seems heavy.

Spoon it into a greased Bundt pan. (Tap the pan on the counter to get out air bubbles and even up the batter.) Bake for approximately an hour, or until the cake starts to pull away from the edges of the pan.

Let cool completely then invert onto a cake plate. Zest a lemon and enjoy that most fragrant experience.

Spoon frosting into a microwaveable pitcher or bowl and heat for about 12-15 seconds. Pour liberally over the cake, letting it drizzle down the sides. Sprinkle a little lemon zest over the top and garnish with strawberries, if desired.

Author's Note

Thank you for coming along on another adventure in Holiday. It was fun to give Ruth and Matilda another opportunity to use their matchmaking skills. I hope you enjoyed the story and their antics.

I was driving home from town one day, flipping through radio stations when a country song that was popular years ago started playing and made me laugh. The old Joe Nichols song asks the question, "What's a guy gotta do to get a girl in this town?" I loved the idea of the hero asking that question as a way to start this story. I could just picture Justin struggling to find suitable dates and hoping the men he worked with could help. Instead, their teasing and tormenting left him frustrated (but made for some fun writing!). If you've ever lived in a small town, you know what it is like!

Not long after I released *Valentine Bride* (the first book in the Holiday Brides series), Captain Cavedweller and I had gone to the big city and were driving down a busy street. A small hatchback car in front of us was packed to the gills with foam coolers bearing the American Red Cross logo.

As we drove behind it, we contemplated what might be in those coolers and decided it might be someone who'd collected donations from a blood drive. Then, when that car narrowly missed being hit at an intersection, the idea popped into my head with the tomato-soup accident. (I had to use tomato soup. I just couldn't make it be real blood.) So that's where the inspiration for the soup in Sage's accident came from.

Speaking of Sage's accident, another real-life experience played a part in the teen driving through the stop sign because she was texting. Back when I was a recent college graduate and had just started my first "career" job, I bought a brand-new Chevy S-10 pickup. I loved that little truck. It was what I drove as I learned about being a journalist and traveled all over our county writing stories. It was often the vehicle Captain Cavedweller and I took when we had a date. In fact, we both drove that pickup for the next twenty years. We might still be driving it if it wasn't for a texting teenager.

Captain Cavedweller had the day off and was going to run into town to meet me for lunch. He took a back road that curved around a steep hill with a sheer drop off. He'd just started up the hill when a big dually-tired tractor started down the hill. Then the tractor crossed the center line and kept coming toward him. He couldn't swerve around it, so he finally pulled over next to the guard rail (with that sheer drop off below him), and stopped. A teen girl was so busy playing with her phone, texting someone, that she drove the tractor into our pickup and pushed it into the guard rail. We still are so grateful and feel so blessed that the guard rail held and Captain Cavedweller wasn't injured. Tire tracks marred the entire driver's side of the vehicle, but it didn't even break the glass in the windows. Our poor little pickup was totaled, but I do hope the girl learned a valuable lesson about not texting and driving — even in a tractor.

The candy and popcorn Justin mentions in the

story is inspired by a company headquartered in Medford, Oregon. If you've never heard of Harry & David, I encourage you to give their Moose Munch a try (or the truffles!). Your taste buds will thank you.

One day while Captain Cavedweller was trapped in the car with me on a drive into town, we were talking about old television shows he watched as a kid and he mentioned The Greatest American Hero. The show was cheesy (but pretty awesome to a pre-teen who loved superheroes) and had a great theme song. It seemed perfect for Sage to set that theme song as her ringtone for Justin.

Crosby the cranky, crotchety, persnickety, neurotic, freak-a-doodle feline is entirely inspired by our cat, Drooley. Not only does Crosby get his fear of everything from our nutty feline, he also got Drooley's bad habit of standing in his water bowl, lapping out of the faucet, and wanting in the garage to eat.

The scene about the mouse hiding in the garage and packing food for the apocalypse... happened with our deranged cat. Captain Cavedweller and I take turns feeding the cat — in the garage, of course. We'd both noticed his food bowl was unusually clean but didn't think much of it until CC said something to me about noticing not a crumb remained in the cat's bowl. We compared notes and discovered the dish had been licked clean for about a week. Highly unusual behavior for our loony cat.

CC set a bunch of traps around the garage and near the food bowl, but didn't catch anything. So we did a major cleaning in the garage and couldn't find a nest, or any evidence we had an interloper in our midst. We even looked in our furnace room, but, like in the story, nothing looked or smelled amiss. A few more days and empty cat bowls later, I finally decided to dust the garage floor with flour and see what kind of tracks turned up. The next morning, both CC and I hurried into the garage to see what we could find. There were footprints all around the food bowl, heading toward the furnace room. They looked far too big to be a mouse, though, so we had visions of it being a big, gnarly-fanged rat. CC had to get to work and there was no way I was dealing with the rat alone, so we decided to tackle the project the next day.

That night, we caught a ginormous mouse in one of the traps. And yes, it was a mouse, just a huge one that was super fat from all the cat food he'd been swiping. We still couldn't figure out how one mouse (even as big as he was) had eaten that much cat food. I opened the furnace room door, and again didn't see anything amiss. And it certainly didn't smell like we'd been invaded by a nasty rodent. I began to move a few things around and a little trickle of cat food appeared from behind a suitcase.

When I moved both suitcases, we discovered where the mouse had squirreled away pounds and pounds of cat food.

Not only was there this huge pile of cat food, he'd managed to push it between the edge of the concrete and the wall, and solidly packed it beneath a set of shelves. In the time it took me to turn around and get a shovel and the garbage can, our crazy cat raced in, chowing down on the mouse-slobbered cat food like he hadn't eaten in years.

I'm still not sure what's worse: the fact the cat is too scared of a mouse to catch it, or that he prefers his cat food with mouse slobbers.

I can't end this note without expressing my gratitude to Shauna, Katrina, Leo, and my beta readers. You are all so awesome. And a big shout-out to Peggy L. for coming up with the name of Fred Asteer. Makes me smile every time I type it, so thank you, Peggy!

My sincere thanks to you, dear reader, for reading another *Holiday Brides* adventure. I hope you enjoyed meeting Justin, Sage, and Shane and getting to read more about Matilda and Ruth. If you have any characters in mind for future stories in this series, please let me know!

Best wishes!

Thank You

Thank you for reading *Summer Bride.* I'd be so appreciative if you'd share a *review* so other readers might also discover adventures of Baker City Brides. Even a line or two is appreciated more than you can know.

If you liked reading about the town of Holiday, be sure to check out all of the Holiday Brides books!

Holiday Express
Four generations discover the wonder of falling in love and the magic of one very special train in these sweet romances.

Also, if you haven't yet signed up for my newsletter, won't you consider subscribing? I send it out when I have new releases, sales, or news of freebies to share. Each month, you can enter an exclusive giveaway, get a new recipe to try, and discover details about upcoming events. When you sign up, you'll receive a free digital book. Don't wait. Sign up today!

And if newsletters aren't your thing, please follow me on BookBub. You'll receive notifications on pre-orders, new releases, and sale books!

Easter Bride *(Holiday Brides Book 3)* — Piper Peterson loves the small community of Holiday, Oregon. She resides there at a beautiful, old farm where she's surrounded by animals she's rescued. And she manages the feed store that's been in her family for more than a hundred years. Despite her contentment with life, her grandfather's plans to sell the store and farm leave her future up in the air. When a sly matchmaker works to set Grandpa up with the perfect woman, Piper jumps at the chance to lend a hand. But the last thing she expects is to fall in love while helping her grandpa find happiness.

Stuck at a crossroads in his life, Colton Ford can't decide which direction to head. Then an invitation to stay at his brother's ranch in Holiday provides an opportunity Colt can't pass up. He hopes time spent at the Flying B Ranch will help him clear his head and sort out his life. Before long, he finds himself entangled in a matchmaking plot involving his widowed aunt and a charismatic old gent. When he agrees to give the budding romance a nudge, he has no idea the man's delightful granddaughter will capture his heart.

A heartwarming story filled with country charm, laughter, and hope, Easter Bride is sure to bring readers the joys of budding spring and sweet romance.

Turn the page for an excerpt...

Easter Bride Preview

Cold air that felt like it blew straight off arctic ice caps wound around Piper Peterson's neck, in place of the scarf she forgot to grab on her way out the door that morning.

The frigid sting added haste to her steps as she hurried across the back parking area at Milton's Feed & Seed to the employee entrance. The keys in her hand might as well have been shards of ice as the cold metal stung her bare hand. Fingers fumbling, she shoved a key into the lock and opened the door.

Automatically, her hand reached to the right and flipped three switches, bathing the store with light.

"What is the deal?" she muttered to herself as she unlocked the door to the office and hung up her coat. The past two weeks the weather had been in the high forties. One day it even hit fifty-degrees. Then she awoke this morning to temperatures in the low teens, frozen stock tanks, and grumpy animals waiting for their breakfast.

She couldn't blame her collection of four-footed friends for being out of sorts. She wasn't too keen on the idea of a cold snap, either.

Piper turned on the computer in her office then put on a large pot of coffee in the front of the store so customers could enjoy it, too.

While the coffee brewed, she wandered up and down the aisles making sure the two high school students who worked the closing shift had tidied shelves, swept the floor, and cleaned the bathrooms.

Satisfied everything met her high standards, Piper walked to the front of the store and allowed her gaze to roam over the framed photographs hanging on the wall behind the cash registers. Some of the images went back to the late 1800s, when her great-great-grandfather, Randall Milton, opened the store.

Back then, the business was a livery and blacksmith shop that offered feed and tack supplies on the side. The store changed with the times, but a guarantee of friendly, honest service remained the same through all the years and generations of Milton men who'd owned and operated the store.

With no men left to carry on the tradition, her grandfather decided to sell both the store and his home. He'd retired, hired a manager for the store, and started searching for a buyer. Four years later, he still hadn't found just the right buyer, even though he'd had plenty of offers.

Until her grandfather met a buyer he liked, Piper was proud to be in charge of the store and her grandfather's farm. If she had the money available, she'd buy both the farm and the business in a heartbeat, but that was a pipe dream. Up to the moment her grandfather turned over ownership to someone new, though, she intended to make Milton Feed & Seed the best feed store in Eastern Oregon.

She returned to the office, went through incoming emails and sent out several, reviewed the receipts from last night, and prepared the deposit to take to the bank.

Those business classes Grandpa suggested she take while she was earning a veterinarian technician degree sure came in handy.

Even if she hadn't taken them, she'd spent enough summers in Holiday working at the feed store to know every detail of the business. She was grateful her father had allowed her to spend her summer vacations with Grandpa. She loved the small town and there was nothing quite like being with her grandfather. As his lone grandchild, and he her only living grandparent, they had a special bond. At least she liked to think they did. She was certain her grandfather would say the same thing.

Piper glanced at the clock on the wall above the desk, grabbed her keys, and headed to the front of the store. She unlocked the door, shoved the keys in the pocket of her jeans, and poured a cup of coffee.

Armed with it in one hand and a duster in the other, she dusted the front counter and around the merchandise on the end cap near the registers.

She turned to look behind her at the store. The center aisles held items people tended to use year-round like leather gloves, rubber boots, and tools. To the right were feed supplies, tack supplies including a few saddles made by a local craftsman, and pet supplies. To the left were racks of western and work clothing including everything from onesies for babies to cowboy boots and belts to western jewelry. She also had two aisles filled with western-themed toys, home décor, and gift items.

Piper stepped into the area that greeted customers when they walked inside the store. She liked to set up seasonal displays there. Not only did it capture their attention and garner sales, it was also a great way to call attention to the beautiful hardwood floor, original to the store. She cherished the fact it had been restored and preserved. Each time the old boards creaked beneath her boots it made her smile.

She took a deep breath, inhaling the scents of coffee, linseed oil, and leather. The store had smelled the same as long as she could remember. She never wanted it to change. There was so much history there, even if the building had been expanded to meet the needs of a growing business over the years.

The small feed and tack shop Randall started had been enlarged in the early 1920s and then completely renovated in 1940, prior to the war. When her grandfather took over the business in the early 1970s, the store was updated again. Then, just five years ago, Grandpa had given it a major facelift. From the outside, the store looked like a big, modern barn with easy-care camel-colored siding and a green metal roof. Inside, the store retained the charm and character that only an old building could offer. Many of the shelving units and display tables were antiques that had been there for decades. One big wooden hutch, with shelves and drawers, had been in use since 1901.

And she loved every square inch of it.

After another long sip of her coffee, she set the cup on the check-out counter then went to the storage room at the back of the building to retrieve a shipment that finally arrived yesterday. She'd ordered items for a Valentine display but they'd gotten misplaced in transit. It took her weeks to track down the order, but at least it arrived before Valentine's Day. She still had ten days to sell the merchandise and planned to get rid of it all.

She'd asked Hailey and Ryan, her two evening employees, to make sure the display area was empty of stock and clean so she could work on it first thing this morning. The two teens had also priced all the new merchandise, so it was ready to set out.

With a vision of exactly how she wanted the display to look, Piper hauled decorations she'd set aside to the front of the store. From the array of items tucked into boxes and storage tubs in the storeroom, she didn't think anyone in her family had ever gotten rid of anything they thought might be useful in the future. Right now, she was glad of that fact.

Groaning beneath the weight of a child-sized bright red 1950s Chevy pickup, she managed to maneuver it onto a flatbed hand-cart and haul it to the front of the store. Once there, she debated how she'd get it on the sturdy display table made of reclaimed barnwood.

If she had to lift that thing by herself, she could almost envision explaining to the doctor at the emergency room how she'd ruptured her spleen or ended up with a hernia. She ran through a list of people she could call to help, but most of them were already at work for the day. She certainly wouldn't ask Grandpa to give her a hand. Not at his age. In spite of his military bearing that came from years in the Army, his white hair and slower steps reminded her he was in his eighties.

The bell above the door jingled and Piper turned to greet the first customer of the day. Recognition broadened her smile as she welcomed a friend.

"Well, if it isn't Carson Ford. I haven't seen you since before Christmas. Did you enjoy the holiday?" she asked. "Weren't you and Fynlee expecting all your family to join you?"

The rancher made a beeline for the coffee pot set up near the cash register as she talked and poured a disposable cup full of the hot liquid.

"We had a great Christmas," he said after taking a sip of the coffee. "It's our first Christmas as a married couple and we thought it would be fun to host a big family gathering for my folks and three brothers, along with Aunt Ruth and Fynlee's grandmother at the ranch. It turned out to be a wonderful holiday. One of my brothers decided to stay."

"Oh, that's great. Is he still here?" Piper asked as she moved two smaller display tables closer to the big display table.

"He is. He wants to work on the ranch through the summer to see how he likes the area. Colton never spent much time visiting the Flying B like I did when we were kids, but he needs time away from the family ranch. This will give him a good opportunity to figure out what he wants to do with his future."

"It's nice of you to give him a place to stay and a job at the Flying B." She glanced over her shoulder at the rancher. "If he needs extra work, I'll be hiring seasonal help in a few weeks."

"I'll let him know." Carson took another drink of his coffee. "What about you? Did you and your grandfather enjoy the holidays?"

"We did, although he seemed to be pining for a certain sweet woman while she was out at your ranch." Piper shot him a teasing smile. "Grandpa is quite taken with your aunt, even if Ruth doesn't realize it."

"Oh, I think Aunt Ruth is well aware of his interest. It's what she plans to do about it where things get hazy." Carson grinned. "We all think Rand is great and she practically beams whenever his name comes up. Just give her some time. When she's ready, Rand can sweep her off her feet."

Piper laughed at the image of her grandfather playing a dashing hero at his age. Stranger things could and did happen, though. She looked back at Carson as he took another drink of coffee. "So what brings you into town this morning?"

"With that storm we're supposed to be getting later today, I decided I better get a load of feed before it snows. I parked the pickup back by the loading dock," Carson said. He took another long drink of the coffee then held the cup up and grinned. "That sure hits the spot on a cold morning. You'd think after such a mild winter we'd be heading into spring now that it's February, instead of dreading a blizzard."

Piper nodded her head. "I'm hoping the weatherman is wrong and the storm will pass right on by, but it sure is cold out there."

"It certainly is." Carson refilled his coffee cup and leaned back against the front counter. "How's your new rescue project coming along?"

Piper smiled at him. "Charlie is doing quite well. Just yesterday, he ate a carrot right out of my hand."

"That's great, but be careful around him," Carson cautioned. "He's a big horse and I'd hate for you to get hurt out at the farm with no one around to help you."

"I am careful, but I feel bad for Charlie. His hooves are a mess. I had the local farrier come out, but he took one look at Charlie and refused to work with him. I haven't been able to find anyone who's willing to do the job."

Carson gave her a studying glance then took another sip of coffee. He tipped his head toward her. "I might know someone who could help you out. If you think Charlie can wait until this weekend, I'll see if he's available."

"I don't think a few more days will make a whole lot of difference at this point, considering everything Charlie has endured."

Piper had a soft spot for animals that was a mile wide and twice as deep. Frequently, she took in animals in need of a helping hand. Most often, she nursed them back to health then found good homes for them. Since moving to Holiday last year to take over managing her grandfather's store and keep up the house and farm until it sold, she'd slowly been collecting animals she couldn't bear to send to a new home.

Right before Christmas, she'd been driving down a

back road after delivering a load of feed and saw a blue roan draft horse in a mud-bogged pasture. The Belgian, with his black mane, tail, and legs, would have been a showstopper if he wasn't coated in mud with large scabs across his sides and back. Ribs poked out, testifying to a lack of care from his owners.

Piper gave no thought to her own safety as she drove down the driveway and knocked on the door of a house in need of paint and a yard that looked like something from a horror movie with rusty junk, rolls of twisted wire, and some scary looking tools scattered around in the dirt where there had probably once been grass.

A sour-smelling man with beady little eyes and stained teeth answered the door. When she asked about the horse, he spewed a stream of tobacco that landed just shy of her foot along with a torrent of cuss words about his ex-wife that made Piper's ears ring just thinking about them.

"That ignorant horse ain't worth the feed I've been pouring into him. If you want that rotten beast you can have him!" the man yelled, then slammed the door.

Obviously he hadn't been feeding the horse and goodness only knew how the poor animal ended up covered with cuts, but she had no opportunity to question him.

Piper didn't give the man a chance to change his mind. She rushed home, hitched her pickup to her grandpa's horse trailer, and returned to the farm. Much to her surprise, the man came out with papers for a horse named Charleston Tango and signed ownership over to her. She thanked him then set about loading the big animal. It took her an hour of patient coaxing to get him inside the trailer, but she'd finally done it. On the drive to her farm, he kicked the sides and made such a racket, she thought he might end up wrecking the vehicle before she made it home and released him in a small pen by the barn.

The horse snorted and reared, and nearly kicked her in the head once before she got him fed and watered. The next morning, she had the vet come out and attempt to doctor his wounds. The vet had to give him a tranquilizer to clean him up, but the deep cuts hadn't become infected and were now well on their way to being healed. Once the blood and mud had been washed away, Piper realized she had a truly gorgeous horse in her possession.

After six weeks, she'd made great progress with Charlie, as she decided to call him, even if he still had trust issues. Who could blame him? She wanted to have the man who'd abused the animal arrested, or give him the same treatment he'd given the poor horse, but she was just glad she'd been able to rescue Charlie.

"It's a good thing you do, Piper Peterson. Not everyone would be willing to risk life and limb to save an abused animal," Carson said, giving her a smile then tossing his empty coffee cup in the trash. He pointed to the red truck on the flatbed cart. "Need some help with that?"

"Oh, do you mind?" she asked, relieved to have an offer of assistance.

"Not at all. Where do you want it?" Carson removed his coat and laid it on the counter then walked over to the truck.

"Just on this table," she said, placing her hand on the big display table beside her. "Once it's on there, I can roll it into place."

"This thing is probably worth a small fortune," he said, straining as he hefted the little pickup off the cart. Piper grabbed the back end and Carson shifted to the front. Together they set it on the table and released a collective breath of relief. "Where'd you get it?"

"Grandpa has had it for as long as I can remember. I think his dad got it in some promotion they ran when the pickup rolled off the assembly line back in the fifties."

Carson's eyebrows raised and he grinned. "And you're going to set it out here for anyone to try and steal?"

She laughed. "As you just noted, it weighs a ton and no one is going to be able to walk off with it. Like the other vintage items on display, it isn't for sale. Everyone who works here knows if there isn't a price tag on something to ask before selling it."

"Your grandpa sure has a lot of neat antiques." Carson looked around the collection of Valentine merchandise she had piled in shopping carts and spilling out of boxes on the floor. "Valentine's display?"

"Yep. My shipment of merchandise was lost in transit but finally arrived yesterday. There's still time to sell it all." She glanced at him as she filled the back of the little pickup with heart-shaped boxes of decadent chocolates she ordered from a manufacturer in Seattle. "You wouldn't be in the market for any special Valentine's gifts, would you?"

Carson smiled. "Fynlee and I married a year ago on Valentine's Day, so I've already got a special anniversary present for her, but I haven't picked out something for a Valentine's Day gift. Any recommendations?"

Piper showed him several pieces of silver heart-shaped jewelry she'd just gotten in, suggested a few ideas based on what she knew about his wife, and offered to gift wrap his selections when she tallied up his bill for the feed.

"It will just take me a minute to wrap this up. Do you prefer pink or red paper?" she asked, picking up his gift selections.

"Definitely red for my Rosie Red." At her

questioning glance, he grinned. "That's my nickname for Fynlee."

"That's so sweet. Red it is."

She turned away from the front counter to a long plank shelf attached to the wall behind it where there were rolls of wrapping paper and spools of ribbon. When she'd been moving things around in the storage room last week, she'd found a new roll of pink paper with little pastel flowers that would work through Easter along with half a roll of red paper dotted with tiny white hearts. After she wrapped the box holding Carson's gift for his wife, she tied it with a white ribbon and fastened on a red silk rosebud.

"Here you go," she said, handing the box to the rancher.

"That looks really nice, Piper. Thank you." Carson took the box and started for the door, then snapped his fingers and turned back around. "I better get something for Aunt Ruth and Grams while I'm at it."

"Of course. What do you think they'd enjoy?" she asked, pulling more merchandise from boxes on the floor to show him.

Carson made his selections, waited while she wrapped the gifts, then took the paper shopping bag she handed to him with his purchases.

"Thanks, Piper," he said, heading toward the door.

"Thank you for your help and spending your money here this morning," she said with a grin. "Tell Fynlee I said hello."

Carson nodded. "Will do. And if the person I know is willing to take a look at Charlie, I'll send him out to see you Saturday morning."

"Great! I sure appreciate it, Carson. Stay warm out there."

He raised a hand in a departing wave before he stepped out into the cold and the door shut behind him.

Piper was busy for the next hour with customers who braved the cold and came in to shop. Her assistant manager, Jason, arrived at ten and took over waiting on customers while Piper tackled the Valentine's Day display. When she finished, she stepped back and gave it a critical eye. In addition to the red truck with a bed full of candy boxes, she'd placed red, white, and black metal stars around, hung up a banner made of burlap with red felt hearts, and set a few red and white graniteware pieces around. She stacked little wooden signs with love sayings, red and pink candles, and inexpensive pieces of jewelry on a tiered metal stand. Red and white painted mason jars left from Christmas now had jute tied around the tops with pink ribbon roses and hearts glued to the string.

Jason helped her carry two mannequins to the display area and she dressed them in dark jeans with red shirts. The male mannequin wore a black vest with a black wild rag around his neck while the female had on a cream sweater with a fluffy cream-colored scarf. After setting cowboy hats on the heads and dangling a leather bag bedazzled with a rhinestone heart from the female mannequin's hand, she tucked more candles and red, white and pink items, like boot socks and gloves, into the display. To finish the presentation, she wrote "Shop in the Name of Love," on a chalkboard and placed it front and center where anyone entering the store was sure to see it.

The bell on the door jingled and she looked back at the customer with a happy smile.

"What do you think, Grandpa?" she asked as Rand Milton made his way to her side and studied the display she'd created.

"Festive. Fun. I like it, honey." Rand wrapped an arm around her shoulders and gave them a squeeze. "You're doing a great job with the store. I'm so happy to have you working as the manager. When Lydia let me know she was moving to be closer to her son and his family in Spokane, I wasn't sure what I'd do. She'd been the manager since I retired. Thank goodness, you were willing to help me out."

"I love being here in Holiday, Grandpa. You know there's nowhere else I'd rather be. Besides, managing the store is fun for me, not work."

"I know, honey, and that's why I'm thrilled you're here. The store hasn't looked this good or had such steady sales in years." Rand gave her another hug then went to get a cup of coffee.

Once he'd taken a long drink, she motioned for him to follow her to the boot section where they could sit and visit a moment.

"What are you doing out on such a cold day, Grandpa?" she asked as she leaned back in one of the chairs people sat in to try on boots, doing her best to ignore the mess someone had made in the children's boots section.

"I heard it's gonna snow and thought I'd get out and around while I still could. I hate being cooped up inside." He glanced at her. "Guess you inherited that from me."

She smiled at him. "I sure did. Mom never enjoyed the great outdoors all that much, at least from what I remember."

A wistful look passed over his face. For a moment, he seemed lost in memories of his only child who'd died from ovarian cancer far too young. "Your mother was always trying to be a little lady. She loved to throw tea parties for her dolls and friends. I think you get your talents at doing crafty things and decorating from her, even if you've always been a tomboy at heart."

Thoughts of her mother, how much she missed her, made Piper's heart ache, so she abruptly changed the subject. "Carson Ford was in this morning. He mentioned one of his brothers decided to stay at the Flying B for a while. Have you met him?"

"The brother?" Rand asked with a teasing smile. "Why? You interested in him? I thought I heard you had a date Friday night with the Guthry boy. If you don't get busy and find a husband, how can I hold onto my hope of having a great-grandchild to hold someday?"

"I did go out with Grady Guthry, but we're just friends, so don't go picking out colors for a nursery." She scowled at her grandfather. "Just to clarify, I'm not interested in Carson's brother. I wondered what he was like. That's all. And if you're gonna be ornery, I'll ask you how Ruth's doing. Got a date with her yet?"

Rand glared at her. "You know very well how things with Ruth are going — nowhere. That woman... Oh, she frustrates and fascinates me so." He released an exasperated sigh.

Piper laughed. "She'll come around one of these days, Grandpa. Don't give up."

"It doesn't bother you that I'm interested in someone who isn't your grandmother?"

Piper shook her head then placed a hand on her grandfather's shoulder, giving it an affectionate pat. "Not at all. Grandma's been gone almost eight years. I think it's awesome someone caught your eye. You deserve all the happiness in the world, Grandpa."

"Thank you, honey." He leaned over and kissed her cheek. "As for Colton, that's Carson's brother, he was at church with Carson and Fynlee twice since Christmas. How did you not notice him?"

Piper shrugged, unwilling to tell her grandfather she'd been so busy watching him watch Ruth, she hadn't paid attention to anyone else.

"Colton and Carson look quite a bit alike, both tall and brawny. From what I've observed, Colton seems like a nice young man."

"How young?" Piper asked as she rose from the chair. Unable to sit idle for long, she went to work straightening the children's boot boxes.

"Oh, I'd guess him to be around your age. Ruth told me the ages of all four boys, but I've forgotten. I think Colton is next in line behind Carson." Rand pointed to an area on the far side of the store, visible through the cross aisle. "Did you order the chicks? Won't they be arriving in a few weeks?"

Piper nodded as she finished straightening the boot area. "Yep. They should arrive on the twenty-fifth. Want to show me how you usually set things up?"

"Sure." Rand stood amidst creaks and groans, drawing out Piper's grin. "Lead the way."

Available on Amazon!

More Sweet Romances by Shanna Hatfield

If you love reading about quirky small towns that would make the perfect Hallmark movie, check out the *Summer Creek Series*.

It took the hearts at home to help
turn the tide of the war.
Enjoy these sweet World War II romances.

About the Author

PHOTO BY SHANA BAILEY PHOTOGRAPHY

USA Today bestselling author Shanna Hatfield is a farm girl who loves to write. Her sweet historical and contemporary romances are filled with sarcasm, humor, hope, and hunky heroes.

When Shanna isn't dreaming up unforgettable characters, twisting plots, or covertly seeking dark, decadent chocolate, she hangs out with her beloved husband, Captain Cavedweller, at their home in the Pacific Northwest.

Shanna loves to hear from readers. Connect with her online:

Blog: shannahatfield.com
Facebook: Shanna Hatfield's Page
Shanna Hatfield's Hopeless Romantics Group
Pinterest: Shanna Hatfield
Email: shanna@shannahatfield.com